The Camel who crossed Australia

The Camel who crossed Australia

Jackie French

Angus&Robertson
An imprint of HarperCollins*Publishers,* Australia

First published in 2008
by HarperCollins*Publishers* Australia Pty Limited
ABN 36 009 913 517
www.harpercollins.com.au

HarperCollins*Publishers*
25 Ryde Road, Pymble, Sydney, NSW 2073, Australia
31 View Road, Glenfield, Auckland 10, New Zealand
1–A, Hamilton House, Connaught Place, New Delhi – 110 001, India
77–85 Fulham Palace Road, London W6 8JB, United Kingdom
2 Bloor Street East, 20th floor, Toronto, Ontario M4W 1A8, Canada
10 East 53rd Street, New York NY 10022, USA

The National Library of Australia Cataloguing-in-Publication data:

French, Jackie.
The camel who crossed Australia / author, Jackie French.
Pymble, N.S.W. : HarperCollins, 2008.
978 07322 8543 2 (pbk.).
Animal stars ; 3
Bibliography.
For primary school age.
Burke and Wills Expedition, (1860–1861) – Juvenile fiction. Camels – Juvenile fiction. Australia – Discovery and exploration – Juvenile fiction.
A823.4

Cover images: boy and camel supplied by Getty Images; Burke and Wills supplied by State Library of Victoria; camel portrait courtesy of Natalie Winter; trees and back cover images supplied by Shutterstock
Cover and internal design by Natalie Winter
Maps by Darren Holt
Typeset in Bookman 10/14pt by Helen Beard, ECJ Australia Pty Limited
Printed and bound in Australia by Griffin Press
60gsm Bulky Paperback used by HarperCollins*Publishers* is a natural, recyclable product made from wood grown in a combination of sustainable plantation and regrowth forests. It also contains up to a 20% portion of recycled fibre. The manufacturing processes conform to the environmental regulations in Tasmania, the place of manufacture.

6 5 4 3 2 1 08 09 10 11

*To those who demand 'why?' and 'where?' and 'how?';
who refuse an easy boredom; who dream
of worlds they can explore via everything from
microscopes to spaceships; to all the Beckers,
Wills, Dost Mahomets and Bell Sings still
at school, who will one day roam the
universe: this is for you.*

The journey to Australia

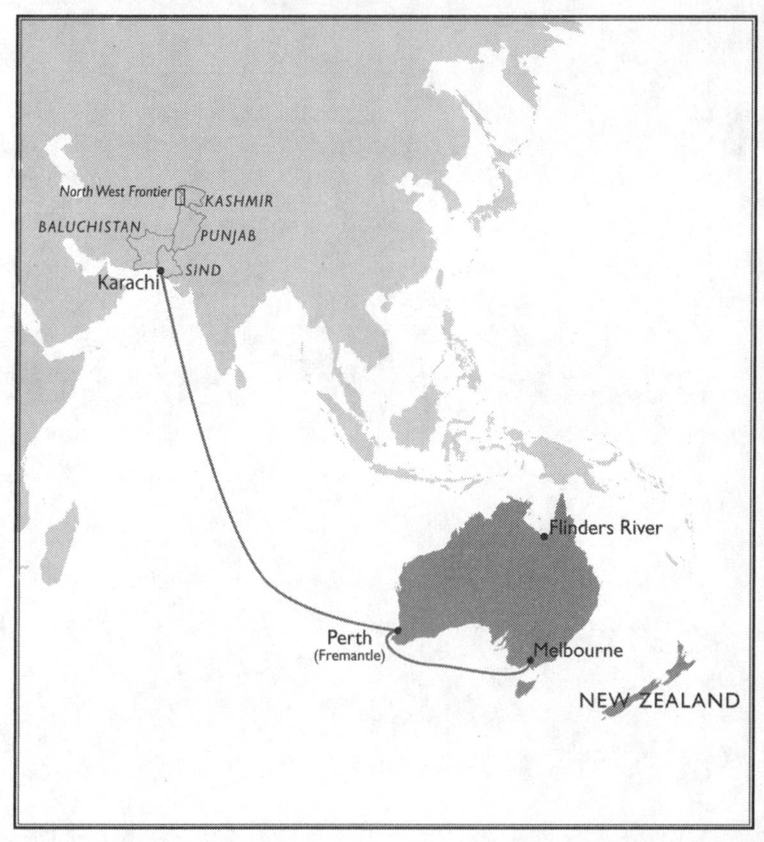

The journey from Melbourne to the Gulf of Carpentaria

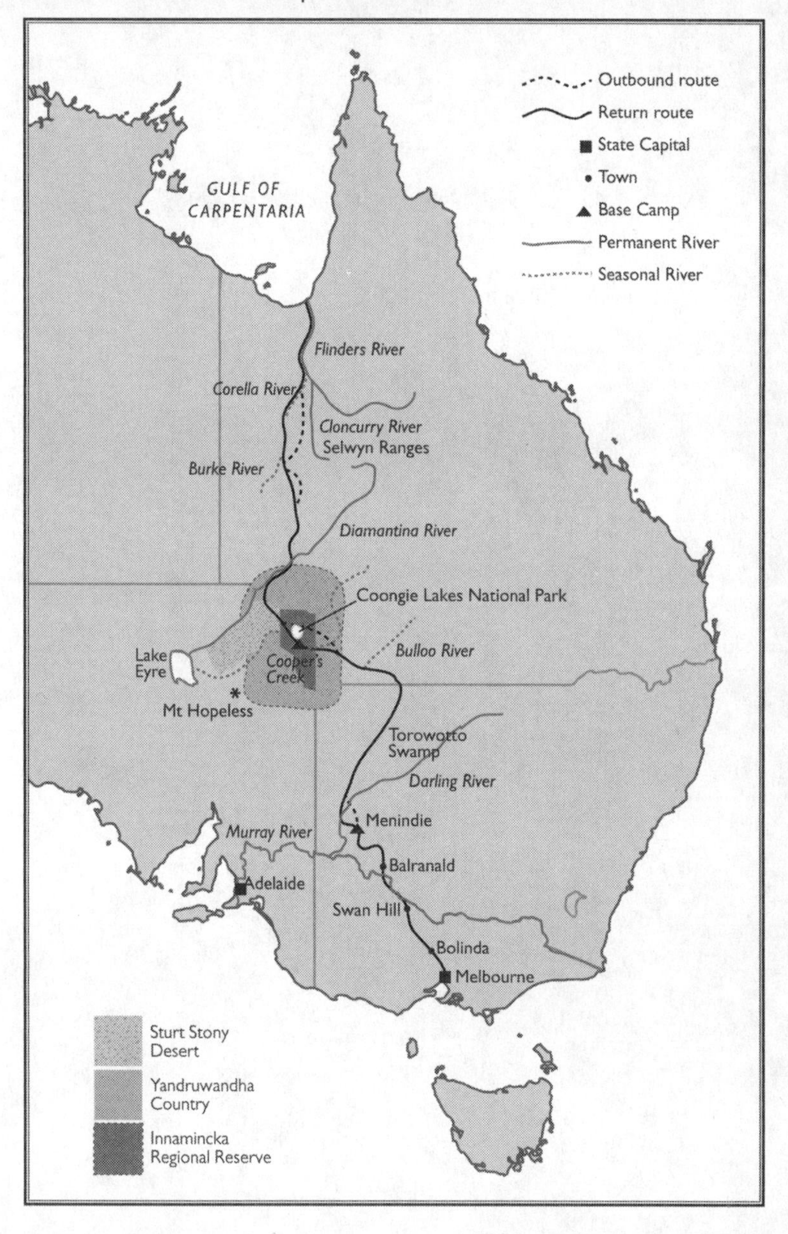

CHAPTER 1

The Camel's Story

Central Australia, 1873

Go away.

CHAPTER 2

The Camel's Story

Central Australia, 1873

Munch, munch, chew, chew ...

You're still here?

Phooey! Phut! You've got sense, even if you're young. I like that in a camel. This is the best spot around.

There's rain coming, too. I can smell it on the wind. This pool may be almost dry now, but in a few days there'll be cool water. The red sand will turn green and be filled with flowers. Ah, the taste of flowers after rain! There's no point plodding across the desert to find grass and good young leaves when you can just wait and let it come to you.

Who are you, then? A bolter? I thought so. They left you unhobbled just a bit too long at your mother's side, and you made a break for freedom? Good for you.

Have you got a name? What did your mother call you? Once I was called Bell Sing. It's to do with the sound of my spit as it lands, and the good groans I make as I rise to my feet. Now I'm *He Who Spits Further Than the Wind.*

Maybe, one day, you'll deserve a name almost as fine as mine.

All right, you can lie down — there, where I can keep an eye on you without moving my head, and listen to your tummy rumblings. You can tell a lot about a camel by the way their tummy rumbles. And their smell, of course. Just make sure you follow my lead if anything disturbs us — dingos, giant goannas, men . . .

What do I know of men, you ask, out here among the stones and sand? Ha! I know all there is to know! I spit upon them! *Phut!*

I'll tell you what, young camel. You lie there, and chew your cud, and learn to smell the sky. What else is there to do while we wait for the clouds to drift in from the horizon, and for the rain to come? And I will tell you how I came to understand the world of men, and how I was once part of the boldest caravan that travelled the furthest in the world . . .

CHAPTER 3

The Camel's Story

Northwest Indian Frontier, 1854

My mother's name was Smelly Breath. What camel could want a better name than that? They said you could smell her half a day's walk away — though I was never that far away from her, not till the end.

My first memory is of standing at my mother's side as I sucked her milk, which tasted as good as her smell. She was a fine strong camel who could carry burdens across any desert, and even up the rocky slopes of mountains.

We were part of a big caravan, along with lots of other camels, though none as rich smelling as my mother, and other animals, and the men and women of our tribe, and their children as well.

Big humans load you with their bundles. Small ones throw stones at you when you're tethered, just to hear you grunt. But they will also share their bread with you, or bring you a tuft of grass. And that is my first lesson to you, young one. Humans are like camels, some good, some bad, though none have our strength or our knowledge of the wind. Some are kind and some are clever, and others stupid as a . . .

Phut. And *phooey* too. There is nothing as stupid as some of the humans I have known.

Munch, munch, chew, chew . . .

What was I talking about? Oh, yes, my mother . . .

My first memory is sucking that good milk till I was full, then nosing round the bushes for something else to taste, just for interest's sake. Then, when I looked back at my mother, there was Bilhari, with his turban on crooked, crouched between her back legs, squirting her milk into his mouth.

Bilhari looked after us. He had two legs, but only one eye, and not as many fingers as other humans either. He smelt more like my mother and the other camels than a man. It is good for a man to smell of camel. It is a far nicer scent than their own.

My mother stood there while he drank. But I was hungry again. I ran up to my mother and nosed between her legs. Bilhari glared at me with his one good eye and shoved me away.

I squealed. I was young and too small in those days to bite him, or kick him, or even spit in his face.

'*Ghhhhrrrhhhh!*' my mother bawled. It was a wail to chill the mountains. She had let Bilhari drink her good milk. But she wasn't going to tolerate a man who pushed her son around!

She galloped forward, leaving Bilhari sprawled in the dust. Then she turned round and charged. She seized Bilhari's arm in her mouth and gummed it, hard.

Bilhari screamed. I scampered with excitement. This was fun!

Bilhari ran a few steps away, as the other men stood around and laughed at the stupid man who had goaded his camel more than she would bear.

Know this, young camel. Men think they rule us, because they lead us by the nose and make us bear their burdens. But a camel needs to make it clear when their rule becomes too much. It was a lesson I would remember all my life.

Grhhmph. Phooey! Munch, munch, munch, chew, chew chew …

CHAPTER 4

The Camel's Story

Northwest Indian Frontier, 1854

In summer our caravan followed the snow.

What is snow, you say? It is cold and wet, neither of which is good for camels.

Snow sits upon the mountains. No, mountains are not like the big red rocks in this desert. They go on and on, and just when you think you've climbed the last one another appears in its place. They reach into the sky, and the snow on top of them is whiter than the clouds.

As the days grew warmer the snow melted into blue-white streams that rushed along the gorges. When that happened our caravan climbed the mountains: we camels and the sheep and humans, and the head man's horse as well.

Horses! *Phut* and *phooey*! I spit upon all horses! I will tell you more about that head man's horse a little later.

The grass and the bushes grew as the snow melted. There was plenty of food for us camels, and for the sheep who travelled with us. What are sheep? Smaller than men and horses, but with four legs, and more hair and even fewer brains.

The spring torrents surged between the rocks and the wildflowers sprang up through the new grass as the weather warmed.

Then as the days grew cooler again and the grass shrivelled in the cold we walked down the mountains, across the rocky hills, then onto the sandy plains, where grass grew only in the wintertime and shrivelled in the summer. For that is life, young camel. There are times when the grass grows, and others when it dies. But somewhere there is always food and water, if you have the wisdom to find it.

Ah, the joy of walking in those days, with the stars shivering in the sky, and the sweet strong stench of the other camels in our caravan!

I liked the mountains, but I liked the deserts more. My feet understood the language of the sand, could feel the vibrations of the other animals that passed. My nose could smell what had been there months before — another caravan perhaps, or a desert fox. Scents flow forever in the desert. You can smell the far horizon and beyond.

The humans walked beside the camels — all but the very small and old, and the head man who rode his horse. Now and then we'd pass a village. It was interesting, peering inside the strange boxes where they lived. But mostly the world was us, and the ground that stretched up to the horizon far away.

We camels led the caravan, of course, all in a line, carrying the tents and the carpets and flour for the bread, the sheepskins and the leather bags.

The men marched at our sides. Then came the sheep, and then the women and children, picking up the camel and sheep droppings to dry for fuel to cook their food and warm them at night. The droppings of a fine big camel like me will burn for half the night.

Sometimes, when the grass and water were good, we would stop for days, till all the grass was eaten and the bushes stripped of their leaves, and we camels had put on the fat again that we'd lost on the harsher treks.

Each morning the humans rose and said their morning prayers while we camels grazed on the grass and the bushes. The women heated water for the drink called tea and ate their hunks of bread, then folded their black tents and the carpets that they sat on, while the men rounded up the fat-tailed sheep.

Then one by one we camels were coaxed to lie down and have their burdens strapped onto our backs.

My mother carried little in those early days, for she was feeding me. I carried nothing at all. I was too small, though it must be hard for you to imagine that I wasn't always the magnificent beast that I am now.

Bilhari milked my mother in the mornings, while she ate the grain and dates he brought her. As we walked more milk came, and at night there was always plenty, even when Bilhari drank some in the afternoons, so I grew large and strong, the biggest and the smelliest of all the young camels in our camp.

Each time another young camel came near my mother gave a special pride-filled gurgle, to let them know that she knew I was so much better than any one of them. '*Grrrrrffffhhhh!*' she called.

Munch, grunt, grunt, chew . . .

What was that? No, I was not asleep, you stupid young camel. I was thinking. Thinking is a good activity, as you will learn as you grow older. The sort of thinking I was doing is called 'remembering', which is when you see things from the past as clear in your mind as if they were happening now.

What was I remembering?

It was a day like this, with a blue sky, no clouds . . . You've never seen a cloud? Well, you will soon, young camel, mark my words. In a few days the sky will begin to dapple and the air will thicken with rain, and after the rain the land will thicken with grass. Ah, it is a fine sight, let me tell you.

But the day I am remembering wasn't like any day you will see here. This day was among the mountain peaks. The rock was so hard that our leathery feet made clumping noises when we trotted on its surface. The air was as dry as it is today, but from cold instead of heat.

The head man lifted up his hand to tell the caravan that we'd stop here for the night. He slid off his horse, who nodded wearily, for he was an old horse. Horses do not have our endurance or strength of character, as well as being . . . ah, well, enough of that.

The men began to untie the tents from the other camels' backs, and the women started fishing in the leather bags for the driest droppings to start their cooking fires.

But my mother sniffed the air. When Bilhari reached for her to kneel so he could untie her packs she gurgled, then she gave a cry. She pushed him hard with her nose, so he tumbled over onto the rock.

Bilhari stood up, quivering with anger, for he hadn't even touched her, or me either.

My mother tossed her head. She flared her nostrils and sniffed loudly. She groaned and butted Bilhari once more.

What was she doing? Trying to talk to a man, of course! Men don't have our sense of smell, and there are other things about the world they cannot sense either.

At last Bilhari worked out what was going on. He looked at my mother thoughtfully. He patted her nice and hard, so the dust puffed out from her hair, to tell her he understood. Then he ran to the head man. I trotted after him, for I was curious. My mother followed too.

The head man glanced up as we approached. He was older than Bilhari, with a long grey beard and grey hair dangling from under his turban.

'What is it?' he demanded.

Bilhari shook his head urgently. 'We can't camp here.'

The head man stared. 'Why not?'

Bilhari shrugged. 'I don't know. But Smelly here won't settle.'

The head man chewed his moustache. 'Smelly doesn't like it, eh?'

'*Fhhhhgggghh!*' my mother gurgled, and stamped her feet.

The head man lifted his hand and addressed the camp. 'Move!' he yelled. He jumped up onto his horse, who had been standing, horse-like, with no idea that anything was wrong.

Everybody stared. But when the head man shouted an order he was obeyed — just as you should obey me, young camel, for I am the leader of *our* caravan.

The men loaded the camels up again. The women put their pots away. The children shouted and scooped up the piles that the animals had left in the short time we'd been camped.

Then we began to walk.

Twice the head man held up his hand to stop again, and twice my mother bellowed and gurgled, so he gave the signal to move on.

The third time he held up his hand my mother sniffed the air. She paused and sniffed again, and thought through her feet, the broad flat camel feet that tell you so much of what is happening and what will happen, once you know how to listen.

Finally my mother bent her head and began to graze.

Bilhari let out a great breath of relief. He signalled to the head man and the head man nodded as his women began to unload his tent.

What was going on? Haven't you worked it out? But I forget, you've never known the mountains or the snow.

Well, then, I'll tell you the rest of the story. My mother had nudged me, right at the beginning, and I listened with my feet as well, so I could recognise the feeling if I came across it again. That is how a camel learns, by watching and listening to his elders.

I hope you understand what I mean.

Well, as I was saying ... we camels began to eat the bushes. The sheep nosed at the grass. Bilhari brought a special handful of dates for my mother, for they were her due, and she ate them while Bilhari patted her side and coughed a little as the dust flew out of her hide. The fires were lit, and the burning droppings glowed like earth-bound stars as the darkness grew.

The wind blew cold that night. Nearly all slept in their tents, except for Bilhari, who liked the warmth of the camels better than his women. The moon began to wander across the sky, just like we had travelled across the rock and sand below.

And then I felt it. Not the faint tremor my mother had shown me how to feel before. This was a shaking that started in my feet, then reached my legs — and then the noise arrived, a roar that filled the world, so that the mountains shook and people ran screaming from their tents.

It was an avalanche. The snow piled high above us on the mountain could no longer hold on to the steep slopes. My mother had felt it trembling. Now it thundered down to fill the valley where we'd stopped the first time! But we were safe, even though our world roared and shook.

I have listened with my feet every day since then, just as I have sniffed the sky. I can tell what will happen, young one, just like my mother did.

For if she hadn't, our whole caravan would have died.

CHAPTER 5

The Camel's Story

Northwest Indian Frontier, 1855 to 1859

They were good years for our caravan. The rains came and the grass grew. The sheep had many lambs. There were many young camels too, though none as fine as I. I was the strongest, the smelliest and the most handsome. I was the best spitter in the whole camp too.

The only bad luck for our caravan was the death of the head man's horse. But he was old and he was just a horse, so I didn't see why the head man was upset. Now every time we passed a village or met a caravan the head man looked at their horses enviously.

I grew taller, and even stronger. I no longer drank my mother's milk, but nibbled the leaves of bushes as we passed, or munched the grass before the sheep got to it (if there is a more stupid animal than a sheep I have never found it). The women squirted my mother's milk into big leather bags, which swung from the luggage as we walked, the moisture oozing out, so that at night there was thick curd cheese for the humans to eat, instead of the good milk. But humans always eat in silly ways. They eat the sheep that eats the grass, instead of nibbling at the grass themselves.

What was I saying? *Grarrrhhha!* I remember . . .

When I was three years old Bilhari began to train me to carry loads. Some camels, as you will have seen, are trained to carry humans, for humans wriggle so much that a camel has to concentrate on them and cannot carry other things at the same time.

The strongest and the best camels, like me, are trained to carry loads. But it is not just strength you need. A load unbalances you. The heavier it is the harder it is not to slip when the ground is uneven, or the way is steep. Many camels fall when the load is too great or the ground is rough. When that happens, *aaaiiii, phut!* A camel can break a leg! He's lucky if he survives.

So Bilhari trained me with just a sheepskin at first, so I could get used to the feel of something on my back, how the weight changed my balance depending on where and how I walked. Gradually he added more weight, and still more.

'He will be the strongest camel in the world!' Bilhari boasted to the head man. But the head man only nodded, for he still mourned his horse.

Finally the day came when I had my nose peg inserted. And that is all I want to say about *that* story.

Why? *Grhhmph!* You stupid youngster! Think what it feels like when you prick your nose on a thorn bush, eh? Now imagine a thick peg being pushed right through your nose, while you scream and roar and men with ropes all hold you down ... For how could they control us, without the pain they cause when they pull upon our reins?

Think yourself lucky you will never have a wooden peg pushed through your nose — not while I lead this mob and take us to safe places, where men can't capture us and inflict indignities and pain upon our persons. And do not ask silly questions again. 'What's it like?' *Grhhmph!*

Yes, well. I accept your apologies.

Munch, munch, munch, chew, chew, chew. Phut!

After a while my nose healed. And because I am the most intelligent of camels, as well as the biggest and the strongest, I soon learnt to follow Bilhari's commands, so I seldom needed anyone to tug at the rein to pull my nose peg and tell me what to do.

Bilhari had been well trained by my mother, too, for a good cameleer is trained by his best camels, just as the camels are trained by him. Bilhari had no need to hobble his camels, as the humans do here. We stayed near the caravan's camp because we and the men were partners. We were happy — except the head man without his horse.

Munch, munch, munch, chew, chew, chew. Grhhmph. I'm thinking again, that's what I'm doing. I am remembering. It is a day I do not like to remember, but it is worth remembering, for it taught me a lesson all of us must know.

It is this: never trust a human. No matter how close you've been to them, even if they admire you and slap your rump to show you off to passers by ... never ever trust them.

I was five years old, the most handsome and the best-smelling camel in the caravan, as I have been telling you. I carried big loads now, many tents and sheepskins. And when our caravan moved each day I walked in front.

Ah, life was good.

And then it changed.

We were down in the hills now, between the desert and the mountains. There were other caravans nearby, for this was a place where humans met, to trade sheepskins and wives, grain and dates, and bangles for the women.

But this morning no one was packing up the camp. Instead the head man and Bilhari walked among us camels.

'We can spare this one.' Bilhari gestured to one of the oldest camels in the caravan.

The head man shook his head. 'We will never get the price of a good horse for him. Now, if we take Bell Sing here . . .'

'Not Bell Sing!' cried Bilhari.

The head man fixed Bilhari with an eye like stone. 'A head man needs a horse! It isn't fitting that I walk while other head men ride. It insults our caravan. And Bell Sing is the only camel here that is worth a horse's price.'

Horses! I spit upon them! *Phut!*

I eyed the two men warily. Humans use a lot of words, and it can be hard to find the meaning underneath.

Bilhari sighed. He gave me the tug that means *Lie down, so we can load you up.*

I groaned, as is proper for a camel who is going to be loaded, just to let the human know the indignity you feel. I did as he commanded, lying on my pedestal, the thick callus that had grown upon my chest, and chewing at my cud while I waited for Bilhari to get on with loading me.

But to my surprise it wasn't the weight of a tent that I felt upon my back. It was just the skins of the sheep we'd eaten at a feast the night before.

I snorted at the smell of those fresh skins, of the blood and meat that had recently been living sheep. But at least the load was light.

Bilhari clapped his hands and I stood up while he grabbed my rein.

And then we began to walk across the rocky hill, the head man and Bilhari and I.

I didn't realise what was happening at first. Hadn't I walked every day of my life, up mountains and across sandhills?

It was only as Bilhari began to lead me down the other side of the hill that I understood . . .

The three of us walked alone. The other camels stayed behind, and the caravan too. My mother, and the black tents, and all that I had ever known.

I would never see them again!

CHAPTER 6

Dost Mahomet's Story

Northwest Indian Frontier, July 1859

At eight years old I first travelled with my father, helping lead our camels laden with sheepskins to sell, or rice, or other trade goods.

At fourteen I married, the bride gold borrowed from a neighbour, though it would be five years before my wife was old enough to leave her father's house.

At fifteen I killed a man, an enemy of the neighbour who had lent me the bride money, slitting his throat from behind as he watched his goats. I cleaned my knife before I put it back into my belt, but left a red rim at the hilt, to remind myself I was now a man.

At sixteen I sat on the blue and red carpet with my father and my uncles as they decided my fate.

Out in the dusty courtyard the women chattered as they ground the wheat for tomorrow's bread, and waited for the leftovers of our meal so they could eat as well. The summer heat shimmered above the mud-brick walls the colour of the hills.

My father reached into the platter before us with his right hand, the knuckles swollen with age and work, and scooped out rice, rich with spices and greasy with goat. My mother was glad to have us home from our last trip. 'It is good money.'

My oldest uncle spat. He had fought the British three times since they had first marched into our land before I had been born. 'Ferenghi money!'

'A river is not dirtied by having a dog drink from it,' said my father. 'The British may be bastard sons of pigs. But they pay.'

I said nothing. I had known what I wanted since the news had leapt from village to village, like goats jumping from rock to rock. A ferenghi was hiring men. But not to fight. This ferenghi wanted men who knew camels.

Men like me.

My father knew what I wanted, too. My father wasn't the oldest of our family. But in the end he'd get his way.

I scooped out more rice as the men talked around me. The ferenghi was offering ten pounds a month, for three years, or four! Clothes too, and blankets, rifle and ammunition. And for all this I would only have to help him buy some camels, then take them to a new land the British owned. We would take the camels in a caravan across the country and back again. So little for so much! Then they would pay me, and pay my fare, and I would come home.

Rich.

I smiled to myself. How like the British sons of dogs, to think they owned a land they hadn't even seen. But money was money, as my father said, no matter from whom it came.

I tried to work out what four years of ten pounds a month would be in rupees while the talk flowed over me. It would be a fortune. Much more than enough to pay back the borrowed marriage gold. My wife would wear gold bangles. I would lend money to others, too. Grateful men would cut the throats of my enemies . . .

'It is settled then,' said my father calmly. He called to the women to come in and fetch the leftovers to eat, and then embraced me. 'We will find the ferenghi tomorrow. We will tell him young Dost Mahomet is the finest camel driver in the world.'

He smiled. His teeth were as white as his turban in the darkness of his beard. 'It is even true.'

I felt warm with pride.

My oldest uncle nodded. 'There are things you must understand about working for the British,' he said. 'I know this, from your cousin's wife's first brother, who the British paid well to fight for them in the war when I fought against them. First of all, they are Unbelievers . . .'

'Dost Mahomet knows that,' began my father impatiently.

Uncle held up a hand for silence. 'And they smell. They do not wash. They use either hand to wipe themselves. Some shave their faces so when their beards grow they look like hairy goats.'

I touched my beard automatically. I hoped it would thicken up soon. I was afraid it too still looked like a hairy goat's.

'They are also ignorant,' added Uncle. 'And stupid when they are drunk. But you must not smile, no matter how silly they are. You must call them "sahib". And when they insult you, as the sons of pigs will do, you must be silent and think of the money you will earn. Always remember that he who can be killed with sugar need not be killed with poison.'

I sighed. Uncle would tell a camel how to spit, and a crow how to tear out eyeballs. 'What is the ferenghi's name?' I asked.

'His name is Landells,' said my father. 'And the name of the new land is Australia.'

CHAPTER 7

The Camel's Story

Northwest Indian Frontier, September 1859

The head man and Bilhari and I kept walking. Soon I could smell men, more than I had ever smelt before. I grew ... no, not afraid. I am never afraid, young camel! But I grew wary, though I was curious as well.

We passed a hill, bare and stony, where many men had done their business. The smell was so strong I snorted and tried to pull away. But Bilhari pulled the lead rope firmly.

And then I saw it: a great crowd of men and animals. There were sheep and goats, camels and chickens, and more humans than I thought could fit into the world. There was dust from all the feet and noise and smells and yelling. It was called a market. And Bilhari and the head man led me into it all.

Chickens clucked from inside sacks and cages. Men chewed chunks of meat. A flock of sheep ran between the stalls. Their rumps were dyed red, to show that they were all from the same flock.

I had to be careful where I put my feet. It was hard to think, with all that noise.

Finally we found a spot by a mud wall. There was no grass, not even a thorn bush to nibble. The dust irritated my eyes too. So when Bilhari pulled my rein I sat down willingly, and shut my second eyelid and my nose to keep out the dust, and regurgitated my cud to chew. Bilhari squatted at my side, looking sad, while the head man eyed the horses at the far side of the market.

Horses! *Phut!* Little wonder I hate them, after what happened to me that day!

Men wandered by, and sometimes a veiled woman with dusty feet. The men stopped to admire me, for I was the most handsome camel in the market, and it goes without saying that a camel is a far more admirable beast than a chicken, a sheep or a horse.

Now and then a man stopped and opened my mouth to check I was as young and healthy as I seemed, then squatted beside us, and asked, 'How much?' But each time the head man answered the man just shook his head and walked away.

The day grew hotter. I swallowed, then brought up some more cud to chew. I waited for Bilhari and the head man to get tired of all this foolishness and take me back to the caravan. The caravan had been my world forever. How could I know what was ahead?

'It's no use,' said Bilhari at last. 'His price is too high.'

Suddenly there was a buzzing at the other side of the market. The head man peered over the bleating sheep and strolling men and women. 'A ferenghi!' he uttered. 'A foreigner!'

I craned my neck to see what all the fuss was about.

It was a man with a strange thing on his head, not a turban like every other man wore, but a thing with a wide rim that I later learnt they call a hat. (Of course you know all about those, young camel.) He wore funny clothes, as well. His beard was long and brown, and his moustaches long and droopy, and his hair straggled from under the weird head covering.

He walked up to us and I discovered he smelt peculiar too. He was with two other men, one young, in a turban and with his beard just beginning, and an older man, also turbanned, with a sword at his side.

The head man nudged Bilhari. They stood up, and Bilhari signalled for me to rise too.

I groaned and muttered. I had just got to my feet when the young man knelt down and felt my legs, then peered into my mouth and eyes. I decided to let him. His smell was good. He didn't rush at me, but treated me with knowledge and the respect due to such a fine camel as I am.

'What do you think, Dost Mahomet?' asked the man in the hat.

'He is a strong camel, Mr Landells,' said the young man.

I grinned, showing my fine camel gums, and spat my cud in Mr Landells's face.

Why? I didn't like the way he smelt. Besides, I didn't want to swallow. You need a peaceful stomach to swallow your cud. There had been no peace for many hours now, so my stomach was upset.

'*Heyyyyyyoop!*' Mr Landells yelled. He wiped my cud from his face, and stared at me.

The young Dost Mahomet patted my side. He spoke again, more urgently. 'He is the best, the biggest camel we have seen. He will carry anything you give him.'

'A fine camel, this,' said the head man eagerly. 'A great, oh, a magnificent camel. And we only want —'

'*Grunt, phooey!*' I interrupted. I began to lie down again and to vomit up another bit of cud.

Bilhari gave me a slap. 'Hup!'

I groaned, prepared to kick him if he tried it again.

Mr Landells pulled a flask out of his back pocket. I smelt the horrid sweet stuff inside as he took a swig before putting it back. But at last he nodded and pulled out pieces of metal. 'That's all we'll need, I think, Dost Mahomet.'

The head man's eyes lit up at the sight of those bits of metal. 'You will not be sorry,' he started to say. 'He is a great camel, a strong fine camel —'

'*Phut, phooey!*' I interjected again.

Bilhari stroked my side. 'You have been a good companion, Bell Sing,' he told me quietly. 'May your way follow the good grass. Go with Allah.'

Then he handed my lead rope to the young man.

CHAPTER 8

The Camel's Story

Lahore, Northwest Indian Frontier, September 1859

Have you ever been hobbled, young camel? Of course you haven't. If you'd been old enough to be hobbled you could never have escaped and come here.

When you're hobbled the humans tie a rope around your front legs and join them together with a short piece of chain, so you can only take small steps. If you try to stride — or run — you fall over.

Hobbling is one of the extreme indignities that a camel ruled by humans has to bear.

The young man took my rope and led me to the outskirts of the market. There were many other camels there, though none as big or fine as I. All had the rope and chains around their legs. But even then I didn't guess what the young man planned to do until he'd knelt and fixed the first rope to my leg.

Was I a village dog that had to be tied?

And so we camels stood there on the outskirts of the market, while hens clucked and humans yelled and bartered. There was no grass. Even the bushes were almost stripped bare. The dirt was hot, the sun was hot. There was no water either. What was going to happen now? I wondered. What new caravan had I joined?

Then I saw Bilhari and the head man, heading up into the hills and back to our caravan. The head man was riding a white horse. *Ha*, I thought. *That animal will probably go lame on the first hard mountain range.* Bilhari clambered up the rocky slope behind him. Neither one looked back as the horse's tail swished at the flies.

Horses! I spit upon them! *Phooey! Phut!*

CHAPTER 9

Dost Mahomet's Story

Lahore, Northwest Indian Frontier, September 1859

I will never forget that first night with Mr Landells and the camels.

My father had told me when I was small that every journey begins with a single step. No matter how long the journey is, one more step is all it takes, and then another and another . . .

This is my first step, I thought that night, as I sat about the fire after the evening prayers to Allah, and watched the sparks flicker in the dark like stars. I had helped the ferenghi buy his camels. He hadn't even known a riding camel from a pack camel, and we had paid too much. It seemed he had money to waste.

There were twelve of us about the fire, eight cameleers, Mr Landells — the ferenghi — and the guards he'd brought from India. But at least the guards were polite, not like the soldiers who had rampaged through our village when I was small.

Mr Landells didn't speak my language, and only a few words of the guards' tongue. But I had learnt a bit of English, trading with my father, enough to make him understand. Ferenghis mostly only know their mother's tongue, my father said. They are too stupid to learn the languages of others.

I looked at the other cameleers, eating their goat meat and bread by the firelight. There were none from my own land. They were as foreign to me as Mr Landells. One wasn't even a Muslim. Simla was a Hindu, a small thin man with a bare chin and wild moustaches that looked like they were trying to fly off his face.

The rest of us were all Believers. Belooch was a stocky man who had worked for the Ferenghis before. At times I wondered if he had been born of camel parents, for there was no camel he could not calm. Esau Khan was from Kalat, tall and wiry, Nur from . . .

I shook my head in the darkness. It was hard enough to remember the names, much less where we all came from. None of us shared a mother tongue, though we could all make ourselves understood in Hindi, and apart from Simla we had the language of our prayers in common, and some English words too.

I had never travelled with men who were not my kin before. But I was finding that once you have sat together in the darkness, each holding a good British breech-loading rifle that Mr Landells had supplied (for who knew who might attack us in the night?), you begin to feel the men beside you are your kin. As old Uncle would say: 'The first day you meet, you are friends. The next day you meet, you are brothers.'

For as long as Mr Landells hired us, anyway. I caressed the rifle on my lap, and smiled to myself in the darkness. I had never held such a fine weapon in my life.

Old Uncle had been wrong about one thing, at least. Mr Landells's beard was so thick an eagle could nest in it. But Uncle had been right, too. Mr Landells knew little about camels. And he liked men who called him 'sahib', and believed he knew a lot.

Nur had been longest with Mr Landells. (He was good at nodding and saying 'yes sahib' too.) Nur told me that despite the ferenghi money it had been hard to hire men. The memories of the British wars were too fresh for fathers to trust their sons to a ferenghi, and Mr Landells had wanted men who spoke some English as well as camel experts. Many Hindus, too, refused to cross the ocean. It had taken Mr Landells more than a year to hire us eight, and to find the twenty-four camels the expedition needed.

'Expedition?' I tried to fit my tongue around the English word.

Nur nodded. 'We will be part of what the British sons of dogs call The Great Victorian Expedition. Mr Landells and Mr Burke will lead this expedition right across Australia.'

'What will we be trading?'

'Nothing.'

I stared at him across the fire. 'Even the British are not so stupid.'

Nur laughed. 'No one has ever been across this country! We will be the first. Other caravans can follow our route, and men can claim new lands for their farms.'

I was silent at the thought. Could there really be a place where no man had trod before? 'But why not use their own camels?'

'The British like horses. But the centre of this Australia is hot and dry, like here. The horses die of thirst. They need camels to cross the deserts — and us to tend the camels.'

Nur's words stirred something deep within me.

An unknown land. A land where no man could go without my aid. I looked at the faces in the firelight and thought: *Together we will find a path across the deserts of Australia. In a hundred years men will say 'Dost Mahomet and his brothers found this way . . .'*

It will be like vanquishing an enemy, I thought, *but this time we will use camels instead of knives. This time it will be the land we conquered.*

Suddenly a camel shrieked behind us. Mr Landells started. 'What the . . .?' he swore. 'Are those beasts trying to murder each other?' He took another swig of rum from his flask.

I stood up. 'I see to them,' I said. I would have liked to explain to him that there is always trouble with new camels at first. Camels are like men. They need to get to know each other. But I didn't have enough English words to tell him.

I grabbed a chunk of bread then slipped beyond the firelight. As my eyes adjusted to the dimness I could see the big black shapes of the camels, shuffling in their hobbles as they reached for the leaves on the bushes. All but two of them, who stood there nose to nose.

Trouble, I thought, as one of them lashed out and tried to gum the other's neck. I smiled in the darkness, remembering my father's words: 'Softly, steadily. Never be rough with a camel, my son. Move slowly but surely with your camels. Speak softly. Then they will know you are the leader, and obey.'

'Shoosha, shoosha,' I said quietly. Both camels turned as I approached.

I recognised them now — the big one that Mr Landells rode, called Rajah, and one almost the same size, a large pack camel called Bell Sing. Even as I watched, Bell Sing tried to savage Rajah again.

I had to separate them. I walked forward and grabbed Bell Sing's lead rope. 'Koosh,' I ordered.

He lunged towards me, trying to gum my arm. I stood back, then gave him a quick tap on his chest to say, *Get back*.

He hesitated. *Ah*, I thought, *someone has trained you well*. This was good to know. I tapped him again. 'Koosh,' I said again, giving him the order to lie down.

He ignored me. But at least he didn't try to bite me again.

'Koosh, koosh,' I said, over and over.

At last he seemed to give in and settled down.

I had made him obey. Now I had to make him my friend.

'Koosh, koosh, big boy,' I said softly. I patted his back, firmly, so he knew I meant no harm, then offered him the bread I had brought from the fire. It was fresh baked that day — one of the guards had bought it from a village woman. I could smell its sweetness in the soft night air.

'*Grgghhmpph*,' said Bell Sing. He gently took the bread in his mouth, without trying to gum my arm too, and began to chew it.

I sat down on the rocky ground next to him, and patted his neck while he chewed. Rajah moved off — I had shown him who was boss here, too. It was comforting, sitting here with a camel by my side.

Bell Sing was quiet now. *I'll have to warn Mr Landells to keep him apart from Rajah tomorrow*, I thought.

Tomorrow, and the tomorrow after that ... We would walk a thousand miles to Karachi, then sail who knew how many miles across the sea. And then the greatest expedition in the world would set out across Australia, carrying me along with it.

An unknown land. An unknown desert. Deserts had swallowed men before, and not even bothered to spit out their bones.

Yes, this was the greatest adventure a young man could ever have. But here in the darkness I admitted I was a little scared too.

CHAPTER 10

The Camel's Story

October 1859

It was strange at first to be in a new caravan, with new camels about me and new handlers too. But it was not so different from the life I'd known before. We walked, we stopped to graze and doze, then the men would load us up again and we would walk and walk and walk.

There were no women to cook the food in this caravan, and no children either. But there were women in the villages we passed, and children who came running after us with their manure bags to pick up our droppings.

Every morning the cameleers took our hobbles off and roped us in a line. This was an insult, as though we camels did not know how to follow the one in front.

But what could I do? My lead rope was tied to my nose peg. Sometimes small things can control big ones — a small wooden peg can control a magnificent animal like me.

I was the biggest and the strongest camel. I should have led them all, as I had led my old caravan. But no, in this caravan Mr Landells led the way on a big camel called Rajah. My groan was twice as loud as Rajah's. I could spit much further too. Rajah could hardly give a proper spit at all, just a *Phht!* that landed only a few feet away.

Mostly the young man who had admired me in the market fed me. His name was Dost Mahomet. He was wise. He realised Rajah was a troublemaker. He made sure that we were at opposite sides of the camp when we were hobbled, so it was too far for Rajah to get in my way. And during the day Dost Mahomet saw that I wasn't tied right behind Rajah either, where I would have had the insult of walking in his dust. Ah, yes, Dost Mahomet had sense, for a human.

And so we walked, carrying the tents and bags of grain and other things, and the humans rode, with Mr Landells sipping from his flask in front, and the cameleers on their riding camels trotting back and forth to check on us pack camels.

At first I could still smell the lands I knew, the soft scents that rose to us on the wind. But slowly those smells faded and everything was new.

I missed my mother and Bilhari. I missed our caravan. I even missed our head man, that stupid man who had sold me for a horse. But most of all I missed the land that I hadn't known I loved till it was gone. I missed the sharp scent of the snow, the spread of sand beneath my feet.

We walked on hard roads now, the dirt packed like rock by many feet and wheels. At night we ate hay, which I disliked at first. But slowly I got used to it. There was no choice, you see. I either ate it or I starved.

And finally we came to A Big City.

You do not know what A Big City is, young camel? I hope you never do.

A Big City is just like a market only bigger — and full of humans, all yelling or chattering away. There are so many houses there is no room for grass. Many vibrations confuse your feet. Horses and cows leave their droppings in the street. Sometimes there are stalls with good things to eat. But as soon as a camel puts his nose into the food someone smacks him on the rump or on the nose.

Our humans got down from their camels and walked through the streets by our sides, to stop the townsfolk from crowding us too much and stop the small boys throwing stones. Why were we here? I wondered. And where were we going, so far from good bushes to chew?

Suddenly I could smell something I had never smelt before.

And then I saw it.

It was a green land but it moved as well — no, do not doubt me, young camel, for all I say is true. It went up and down, and some things sank beneath its surface and others floated on the top.

This strange land was called The Sea and it was made of water like a pool or lake, but so much bigger that it was a different thing, just like a grain of dirt is not a sandhill ... No, do not snicker! All this is strange, but true! You will listen politely, young camel, or not at all!

We camels stood, all in our line, while men bustled past, looking at us admiringly or warily. At last Dost Mahomet brought us water, and then hay.

The sun was hot. My nose ached from the pressure of the peg.

But worse was to come.

Mr Landells clapped his hands. Dost Mahomet reached for Rajah's lead rope, and pulled him forward, which meant the rest of us, tied together, had to walk as well. He led us over planks of wood, onto a big house called a boat, which bobbed upon the sea and smelt of men and salt and rats.

And, oh, the shame of it, the horror. The world went up and down under our legs . . . and even more was to befall us. Now our lead ropes were untied, and we were led down, one by one, into a place that stank of water, rot and horses, with damp hay about our legs.

It was dark down there. Soon it grew darker still for once we were all aboard we heard something overhead slammed shut.

And it was as dark as night, although it still smelt like day.

CHAPTER 11

John King's Story

SS Chinsurah, Karachi, India, May 1860

It was good to be on the ship at last. I leant on the rail on deck and let the fresh wind wash across my face. It smelt of salt and seabirds — not the hot scent of spices and the betel nut the natives chewed.

It was as though I'd been given a new life.

I'd always wanted to be a soldier. No, that isn't true. I'd been destined to be a soldier, and had spent six years at the Royal Hibernian Military School in Dublin. That school made us tough, we guardians of the Empire. We had to be. The Queen's Empire stretched across the world.

'The sun never sets on the British Empire,' Mr Pomfret told us as our pen nibs scratched on the paper on our desks. And, as I sat there, like countless schoolboys before me, I dreamt of the day I would go out there and help rule the Empire too.

Tough, that was what we had to be. But I wasn't. Not tough enough.

I had been for a time. I went to India when I was fourteen, then joined the 70th Regiment. I was only sixteen when I saw my first battle in the Mutiny of 1857, too. Women and children murdered by the natives . . .

I'll never forget that station up in Peshawar. Vultures sat on the grass, among the flowers, I thought at first. Red and blue flowers on the grass. Till I saw that the red was blood, and the blue was a woman's stained torn dress . . .

I learnt more in those few months than I ever had in all my years at school. Learnt to keep going, even when I was sick to my stomach. Learnt to keep what I felt from showing on my face. Learnt never to trust a native, too, by George. They'll smile at you and seem to do your bidding. Then one night the knives will come out.

No, never trust a native.

At sixteen I was a soldier. At seventeen a hero. At eighteen I was useless. No use to the army. No use to anyone.

It was the fever that did it. The Indian climate, the heat, the water. I went up into the hills where the climate was milder. For over a year I rested and tried to recuperate. Go home, they said, when it looked like I would live. The cold of home will buck you up. Go back to England or Ireland . . .

To what? A clerk's job in an office? Sitting all day, making marks on paper?

But what choice did I have?

And then I met the man who changed my life. It was in the Club up in Rawalpindi. He wasn't an officer, or even a gentleman. He was stumpy, with a broad face, and a beard that needed trimming, and a look about him that said he could sell your own horse back to you and you'd never notice. A bit of a rotter, really.

It was my colonel who introduced us.

'This is Landells,' he said. 'Good judge of horses. Sold me that hunter you saw last year. Landells, I'd like you to meet John King. King's up here to get over the fever. Used to be in the army.'

'Pleased to meet you, Mr Landells,' I said politely. I had no interest in the colonel's guests, nor in his horses — it was unlikely I'd ever be able to afford a hunting horse in my life. But it explained why the colonel had brought a man like this to the club. A man who can get you a good horse is invaluable. 'What brings you to Rawalpindi, sir? The horse trade again?'

Landells grinned. It was a lazy grin. It seemed to say, *I know you don't think much of me.* 'Adventure,' he said softly.

I blinked. 'What sort of adventure?'

He laughed, and swallowed his drink in one great draught, then signalled a servant to get him another. 'The greatest adventure in the world, boy,' he said. 'I've been here for a year buying camels, and finding sepoys to look after them. I'm taking them back to Australia for the greatest expedition the world has seen.'

I knew where Australia was, of course. One of the boys I was at school with in Dublin was posted there. Only second raters, they said, went to Australia. Not the place for a man who wanted a glorious career.

Like mine might have been . . .

Landells gulped down his drink, then wiped his hand across his mouth. *Yes*, I thought, *definitely not a gentleman.* 'You've heard of Captain Cook? Richard Burton? Lewis and Clark?'

'Of course.' Who hadn't heard of those famous explorers?

'Well, the whole world will be talking about us next. The Great Victorian Exploring Expedition. We're going to cross the continent of Australia from south to north. The Victorian Royal Society is putting up the money, and a heap of private investors too. Melbourne is one of the richest cities in the world, thanks to the Gold Rush. And they're spending some of that gold on us. No expense spared. Whatever we ask for we get! We're going to make a track though the wilderness. See things no white man ever has before.'

'You're in command?' *Surely*, I thought, *no one — not even colonials in Melbourne — would put a man like this in charge of a big expedition.*

'Second in command. I'm in charge of the camels. We're going to need camels in the places we're going. Too hot for horses. Too rough for wagons, too . . .'

The servant brought him yet another drink. *The colonel*, I thought, *is going to have a large bar bill tonight.* Landells grinned again. 'Want to come with us?'

I gaped at him. 'Me, sir?'

He grinned. 'Why not? The colonel gave a good report of you. Also says you have some experience with camels.'

'A bit, sir. But, sir . . .' Surely he'd seen the hollows under my eyes, the way my hand trembled as I held my drink.

He broke into laughter — so loud that people looked at us. 'The sea air will see you right. And we'll spend time in Melbourne before we set out. You'll be well enough by the time we're ready.'

And here I was, I thought, as I stared out at the sea, and tried to ignore the clatter of the dock behind us. A few hours more and we'd be under sail. A new country, a new life. And maybe a chance to be a hero once again . . .

CHAPTER 12

The Camel's Story

At sea, May to June 1860

We sailed. Sailing is not fun for camels.

Sailing is where you rock and sway, and when you lie down your skin chafes in the wet and rotting hay.

Sailing is where you're hurled into a heap, with bruises and swellings on your legs.

Sailing is where you get hay once every few days, the only time you see the light. Your water tastes of salt and rats, and you only get half a bucketful a day, and none when the sea is rough.

And they tethered me next to Rajah!

I would have kicked him, if the rope attached to my nose peg had been long enough to let me move. But I didn't even have any cud to vomit up so I could spit.

All I could do was ignore him.

It was always Dost Mahomet who fed me. The first few days I tried to kick him or gum his arm, to show I still had my self-respect. But as we kept on sailing I grew weaker. Many times I felt too ill to eat.

Why? I do not know. The sea does strange things to your stomach, for I wasn't the only one who couldn't eat. Even Dost Mahomet smelt weak and ill sometimes. But still he struggled to bring us water, and the hay we couldn't eat.

At times I dozed, though it was hard to do even that. As I slept the ship pitched and the rope tugged on my nose peg.

At last there was only blankness. Perhaps I'd grown so weak I was no longer able to tell what was going on.

And then I felt a nose, pushing at my side. A big and mushy nose. It pushed me from my daze and confusion.

Whose nose was it? Why was it pushing? Suddenly I felt the glare of the light from the open hatch above us, smelt Dost Mahomet there in front of me, holding a bucket of water.

I didn't want to drink. I didn't want to live. But the big nose pushed me again. All at once I realised the water smelt good, that my mouth was dry, that my body craved moisture.

I gulped some down. Then I drank some more. Dost Mahomet stroked my nose. I was too weak to even think of gumming him.

Who was it who'd nudged me, who'd brought me back from that awful place where the storm had sent me? It was Rajah, of course.

Rajah ... It is rare, you know, for two big camels to like each other. You can't have two boss camels in a herd.

But from then on Rajah and I were friends.

CHAPTER 13

The Camel's Story

Melbourne, Australia, 13 June 1860

We only knew we had arrived when the hatch was opened and daylight flooded in and smells of a strange new land, too. Oh, the pain as the light hit my eyes!

Dost Mahomet and the others led us up onto the deck one by one. When it was my turn, my legs trembled so much I thought I had forgotten how to walk. But then I felt his hands fasten something around me and *ahhhhheee*! You will not believe it! I flew into the sky!

Up over the deck I flew, with a big flat rope about my tummy, then over the ship's side and onto the dock. '*Ngggghhhaaaa!*' I bawled.

My feet touched firm ground at last. But oh, how I tottered and groaned. You wouldn't think a superb big camel like me could ever be weak, would you, young camel? *Phut! Phooey!* I thought not. But I was. I was so thin my hump was gone entirely.

I could feel the empty pouch of skin flapping to one side.

All around me men exclaimed — and laughed at us too. I would have spat at them if I'd been stronger. Dimly I heard Dost Mahomet argue with the other men, saying we camels must rest till we could see and walk safely.

'*Grrnnnnnftt!*' I moaned. Rajah groaned beside me. It was comforting to hear him next to me now, to smell his special camel stink.

Suddenly Dost Mahomet's hand guided me to sit down, so I could rest upon my pedestal on the wood thing they called a wharf.

Oh, the shame of it, the horror — to be so helpless in front of humans — to sit there unable to even spit or chew my cud!

Then I felt Dost Mahomet's hand again. I was about to try to gum him when I smelt water — fresh water, not the sour old stuff we had been forced to drink on the ship. It was in a bucket, and did not taste of earth and sky, just wood. But it was still better than any I had tasted for a long time.

Slowly my eyes grew used to the light again. I could see!

And what a sight! The big water, and more ships too, and strangely dressed humans, all staring at us, like they had never seen camels before. The other camels looked even thinner than I felt, and more confused and shocked.

How dare the humans poke at us, and laugh at us, as though we were sheep or hens, not camels to be gazed at and admired! I forced my legs to straighten, and even though the world seemed to spin

I managed to stay upright. I bellowed a challenge to the others.

Rajah was the next to rise. He even kicked at a man who peered at us too closely. Oh, yes, an admirable camel in all ways, was Rajah.

One by one the other camels stood as well. The humans cheered. They even smelt different here, I realised — not of spices, but of fatty meat. And they kept standing there and staring.

When Dost Mahomet and the other cameleers knelt down to pray on the wooden wharf the other, pale-skinned humans stared at them as well.

Then the camel handlers tied us to each other again. Oh, the shame and the indignity!

Once more we began to walk. No one rode us now. We were too weak. I think my legs would have failed me if I had had even a single sheepskin on my back.

The streets were hard on my feet, and full of dogs, who do not respect a camel's dignity. There were no good salty bushes to nibble. The air felt cold and damp.

Even worse, I could not see the far horizon, or even smell it, for all the buildings in the way. What use is a place when you cannot smell what is happening far off?

Yet this 'Smelbourne' was not such a Big City as the other one, Karachi. There were no open stalls, either, where a camel could grab a mouthful of dates.

Even worse — oh, much, much worse — there were horses everywhere! Men on horses' backs, horses pulling wagons, big and small. But the horses had to stand back as we were led along. Their owners stared at us — envious, I am sure, and wishing they had a fine camel to ride instead of their miserable little equines. It felt good to be looked at with so much wonder, even if I had to tread between the horse droppings.

Finally we came to a large building, the most gigantic I had ever seen. It smelt of stone, not earth. But it also smelt of — can you guess? — horses! I spit upon them! *Phut!*

But it wasn't too bad. Not after the ship. The straw was sweet and grass-like, despite the stink of horse, and there was water in a trough. There was room to turn around. Even better, I could poke my head over the door and see what was happening, and exchange smells and conversation with the other camels.

It wasn't like being in the open air. Not like sand under my feet and a far horizon to stare at. But after what I had been through, all I wanted was peace and food and rest.

The food came soon. A bucket of grain for each of us and, even better, Dost Mohamet had found some dates! A handful each, but they smelt of home. They were so good I groaned. I didn't even try to gum his arm.

And finally I was able to regurgitate again, and chew my cud, and feel my hump starting to fill up with fat again.

CHAPTER 14

John King's Story

Melbourne, June 1860

To my surprise I enjoyed the voyage. Landells was right. The sea air cured my fever.

It was good to work again, too, keeping an eye on the sepoys, and making sure they cared for the camels properly. Native Johnnies get lazy if you don't watch them.

Melbourne impressed me. I hadn't expected a town of wattle and daub, of course, or army tents. I'd even heard it called Marvellous Melbourne back in India. But it hadn't seemed possible that a colony at the bottom of the earth could possess such grandeur. Many of the buildings were as magnificent as any back home. It was good to see white faces in the streets again too.

But the preparations for The Great Victorian Exploring Expedition impressed me even more. I was one of twenty-two men, with eight sepoys for the camels. Everything possible had been thought of: we would have three big American wagons; tents;

revolvers; oats and potatoes and sixty gallons of rum and pepper for the camels; six tons of firewood; and enough provisions for us for a year. We even had inflatable cushions and cedar-topped camp tables, candelabras, dandruff brushes, a copper bath, lime juice for scurvy and a Chinese gong, as well as a special branding iron with the letters 'B/VE', for 'Burke/Victorian Expedition', so the trees could be branded along the way to show where we'd been. We should be taking thirty camels, as well as fifteen horses. It seemed that Melbourne's gold could indeed pay for anything we needed, and much more besides.

I was impressed with our leader, Mr Burke, as well — and not just because he was a soldier from Ireland, like me, and immediately confirmed the position Landells had offered me.

He was a short, tough-looking man, with a square face under his beard, and long moustaches that he kept oiled and curled. You could tell he'd been a soldier.

There was some muttering — which I carefully pretended not to hear — that Mr Burke had no experience as a bushman, and had never been outside the settled districts. But he had good experience of command, not just as a lieutenant in the Hussars but as a superintendent of police in Victoria. I gathered that for our backers a fellow Victorian was far preferable to the contenders from other states! (And Burke had promised them first claim on any rich farmland we found.)

Seven hundred applications had been received for the other positions in our party, but in the end Mr Burke appointed people that he already knew — a sensible precaution. It is important to have men you can trust at your side.

Landells was second in command, as he had told me back in India. Third in command was William Wills.

I must admit I envied Wills his command. He was young, like me, and small and slight. He'd suffered from fever just as I had. But Wills was a surveyor as well as an astronomer. The expedition had hired him for his scientific skills. We'd need those skills, if we were to find our way across Australia. And I had a feeling Wills was tougher than he looked. He'd been in Australia nearly ten years already, working as a shepherd and a goldminer till he learnt surveying. He'd even studied surgery and chemistry back in England. No, Burke had made a good choice with Wills. It was impossible not to like the man.

I had less in common with the two other scientific officers. They were both Germans, though good enough fellows in their way. Like Wills and the Expedition Committee they believed that new discoveries about the plants and animals, the land and stars, were as important as finding a route across the country.

I couldn't see much point in all that science stuff. But I didn't say so. Science had helped get us the money for this expedition.

Dr Herman Beckler was to be our botanist looking for the new plants that the Expedition Committtee thought so important. Beckler was a doctor too — he'd been working at the Melbourne Hospital when Burke appointed him. Dr Ludwig Becker was a naturalist and our official artist.

He would record the country through which we passed, providing images of the expedition itself for generations unborn. He was grey and balding — too old, you'd think, for an expedition like this. But he'd been a soldier in Rio, and a goldminer in Australia, and he had a way of looking at you as though he could see the sort of man you were as clearly as he could see your face. And with a few lines on paper he could capture the world with his pen.

It awed me to think that schoolboys like I had been might one day look at my portrait and say, 'That man blazed a path across Australia.'

Yes, every aspect of the project was extraordinary. With preparations like that — and an experienced man like Mr Burke to lead us — how could we possibly fail?

CHAPTER 15

Dost Mahomet's Story

Melbourne, 1860

Excitement was building up in me. The voyage had been strange and here in Melbourne it was even stranger.

Back home I could never have imagined floating on a world of water, with sky and sea instead of sand around. Ferenghis stared at us as we performed our prayers on deck. Some had even laughed. I imagined slipping into their cabins in the night, and slitting their throats. But all the time I nodded and was polite, as Uncle had advised. Finally Nur had found us a private place to pray, behind the funnel.

It had been the first time I had eaten non-halal meat, too, for there was no way we could kill and bleed our animals ourselves, as we had done on the way to Karachi. Simla refused to eat meat at all, but Nur reminded the Believers that it is allowed to eat meat that is not halal when there is no other food to be had.

At least now in Melbourne we could prepare our own food again — usually sheep, or one of the stray milk goats that roamed Melbourne, so that Simla could eat with us too. His religion forbade him beef. He was a good man, for an Unbeliever, hard-working and quiet.

Melbourne stank. The rain lingered in the air, as though it wanted to wriggle inside of you. The work was filthy, forking out the hay the camels had fouled.

But I kept thinking of the money I had made already. And soon we would be leaving — we had already been given our blankets, the two pairs of warm trousers and other clothes. Even better, we had been given our rifles back, with as much shot and powder as we wanted, and good knives too, with blades as shiny as a smile.

So I was not unhappy that day when Nur came up to me as I shovelled out the last forkful of muck onto the pile outside the stables.

Nur squatted against a tree. I put my fork aside and squatted down beside him.

'I am going home, Dost Mahomet.'

I stared at him. I knew he didn't like the cold of Melbourne. But to go home, after we had come so far? 'Why?' I asked.

'Why?' Nur repeated in Urdu, the language we both shared. He gazed at me as if I were crazy. 'Weeks in a stinking hold with the animals, while the ferenghis sleep in clean cabins, not on bales of straw like us. And now this place. The wet air will kill us, Dost Mahomet.'

I smiled at him, trying to calm him down as I would an angry camel. 'We will be leaving soon, into the heat and dry.'

Nur shrugged. 'All men must die. But not like this, of wet air and putrid cold. It has given Esau Khan the coughing sickness, and Abdul too.' He hesitated. 'Besides, I do not trust the ferenghis. We have had no wages yet. How do we know they will pay us at the end of the expedition?'

'We have had all he promised so far.'

Nur snorted. 'Don't show me the palm tree, show me the dates. I want to see gold, not ferenghi trousers.'

'Why would they want camels if all Australia was cold like this?' I said patiently. 'And Nur — if you leave now you will not get your wages. Think how much we are owed already. You can't give that up.'

Nur shook his head. 'No. I have decided. So have all the others. A ship to Karachi sails tomorrow, and we shall all be on it.'

I looked at him in dismay. '*All* the others? *Everyone?*'

It would be hard to be alone here, with just the camels. No one to speak my language. No one to pray with or talk to around the fire, as we remembered our families and the mountains of our home. No one else here knew how to care for camels either, I realised with growing alarm. I couldn't do it all myself. Was the whole expedition doomed to fail before it had even begun?

'Belooch and Esau Khan and Simla haven't decided to go yet,' admitted Nur reluctantly.

I felt the breath seep into my body again. Four of us, instead of eight . . . it would be harder work now, caring for twenty-seven camels. But we could manage. 'They won't go. They are men of honour. They have promised and they will keep their word.'

Nur snorted again, sounding just like a camel who doesn't want to rise. 'Promises to ferenghis don't count. They are infidels. Unbelievers.'

'Nur, my friend, I beg you not to go. Think of our fame at home when the expedition returns! Think of the riches we'll have earned, the places we will see.'

'I have seen enough,' said Nur firmly. 'Now I am going home.'

CHAPTER 16

The Camel's Story

Melbourne, 16 August 1860

Day after day crowds of humans came to see us. There was so much racket it was hard to eat in peace. But at least our food was good — as much grain as we wanted and fresh hay, and good sweet water. My hump grew big and firm again. I was able to spit big gobs at the more impertinent visitors now, which was a good thing, as it kept them from getting too near.

It was strange, not being in a caravan, confined in the same place all day. At first I was glad of it, as I was so weak. But as I grew stronger I was bored.

More camels arrived — though none nearly as fine as me, or even Rajah. Young camels were born, which is an event more interesting for their mothers than us males, though the humans shouted happily and made a fuss. We were moved, too, to other stables in a place they called Royal Park. The park also smelt of horses, but had more grass and trees. What use were the grass and trees, though, if we weren't allowed to munch them? Ah, the ways of humans are strange!

Yes, it was weird indeed, that time in Smelbourne.

The days were longer now. I could smell spring not far off. Not the sort of spring I'd known, with melting snows and the desert heat behind them. But I could still smell fresh grass and new green leaves. My mouth watered. I was getting sick of grain and hay.

It was hard just standing there. The wind smelt to me of other places — not just the smelly river, with its stink of humans and other animals, but bushes to explore and fine things to eat, a horizon to walk towards . . . somewhere far away from here.

CHAPTER 17

Dost Mahomet's Story

Melbourne, 17 August 1860

Nur and the other three left straight after we had performed the Salat-ul-Fajr, the sunrise prayer. Mr Landells paid their fares home, as he had kept his other promises. *Surely*, I thought, *Nur is mistaken.* We would get our money too.

It was back-breaking work with just the four of us. But as the days wore on my feeling of excitement grew stronger still.

Soon we would be setting off . . .

It was getting late. The lanterns were being lit around the city. The air was full of the smell of woodsmoke, as women stoked up their fires to cook their husbands' meals. *Even the woodsmoke smells different in this land,* I thought, as I filled another bucket from the pump and began to carry it across the cobblestones. I saw rats scuttle in the corners, chasing fallen grain. One of the new camels moaned in her stall, unused to the confinement.

'You there! Dost Mahomet, isn't it?'

I turned around. Most of the ferenghis treated me with disdain, but this man was smiling at me. It was the young, dark-haired Mr Wills, his eyes gleaming with excitement. *As mine probably are too,* I thought. 'That is right, sahib,' I said as politely as old Uncle could have wished.

He grinned at me. 'I just wanted to have a closer look at the beasts who are going to get us across the deserts.' He peered into the nearest stall. 'Peculiar animals, aren't they? Well, old girl, maybe I'll be riding you soon.'

I shook my head. *Truly,* I thought, *these foreigners know so little about camels.* 'No, sahib. She is a pack camel, not a riding camel. Besides, she calved only last week, so we won't be taking her.'

'No? How about this chappie?'

'That is Bell Sing, sahib. I would watch out,' I added urgently, as a well-aimed ball of spit headed out the stall door. Mr Wills ducked and it just missed him.

'Bad-tempered brute,' observed Mr Wills.

I smiled. 'No, sahib. It is a game he plays, that's all. He will spit at you and groan and try to gum you as you load him. But on the trail he is the hardest worker of all, steady and reliable.'

'Steady and reliable, eh? Good chap.' Mr Wills stretched out his hand. He'd brought an apple, I saw. He held it correctly, on the flat of his hand. Bell Sing wrapped his big lips around it and crunched it happily. Mingled spit and juice dripped down onto the straw. *Perhaps,* I thought, *this Unbeliever is not as stupid as I thought.*

Mr Wills looked at Bell Sing consideringly. 'Well, you may not win any beauty competitions, old fellow. But if you can get us north then you're worth your weight in gold. Or apples, at any rate.' He fished in his pocket and handed Bell Sing another one.

'Sahib, if you please . . .' I hunted for the English words. 'When does the expedition walk?'

'When do we set out, do you mean?' He looked even younger, like a child who couldn't wait to play a game. 'Three days' time. I thought Mr Burke would have told you.'

I nodded slowly, trying to follow all the English words. Mr Burke had told us nothing. He always seemed to be bustling around and yelling. But even though he was an Unbeliever he must be a wise man to have been chosen to lead an expedition such as this.

'Yes, it's all organised,' Mr Wills went on enthusiastically. 'Why, there are even sixty gallons of rum and pepper to revive the camels in the desert. Mr Landells says the camels need their rum.'

I stared at him, not understanding the word. 'Rum?'

'Spirits. You know.' He pretended to pull a flask from his pocket and drink from it.

'Ah, I see.' I hesitated. True, Mr Landells did not know as much as the youngest child in any caravan. But the camels had not been given rum and pepper as we walked to Karachi. What game was Mr Landells playing here? 'Pardon, sahib, but camels do not drink rum.'

'What? Nonsense. Landells knows about camels, old chap.' He pulled a shiny watch and chain from his pocket. 'I'm running late,' he said. 'I'd better go. I just wanted to see the camels, say a proper hello. It was good to talk to you, Dost Mahomet.' He grinned again. 'And you, Bell Sing.'

Bell Sing blew gently through his nostrils. He had brought up more cud and was chewing it thoughtfully.

Mr Wills patted his neck. 'I'll see you again soon, old boy,' he said. 'In a few weeks you and I will have the biggest adventure of our lives!'

CHAPTER 18

The Camel's Story

Melbourne, 20 August 1860

Suddenly things changed.

I had been chewing my cud, musing on my digestion and making a good big spitball to fire at the next human who annoyed me, when Dost Mahomet bustled up, his turban crooked in his hurry. He opened the door to my stall, grabbed my lead rope and led me out.

The other camels were being led out too. What was happening? Were we finally going to join a caravan again, see the wide sky above and feel the good soil beneath our feet, smell this strange new world?

I just hoped they weren't going to load me up too much. A strong fine camel I might be, with my hump its right size again. But I had been so long on the boat, and so long just standing in my stall, that I wasn't sure I could carry a wisp of hay, much less a tent or carpets.

'Koosh!' gestured Dost Mahomet. I lay down obediently, while another camel handler led Rajah up beside me and made him lie down as well.

Hawk, hoff, hoff, coughed the man they called Esau Khan. He coughed a lot, and looked almost as pale as his turban.

One by one we were all brought out and made to lie down so we could be loaded. I waited apprehensively, for the load looked bigger than I had ever carried before — and no camel can carry more than me! But Dost Mahomet argued with Mr Landells, and Mr Landells argued with Mr Burke.

At last most of the luggage was shifted onto the wagons so my load, when it came, was not too heavy, though the shapes above me and the weight felt strange. This wasn't a load of sheepskins on my back, I realised. '*Grff,*' I groaned as I struggled to my feet.

'Right! It's time to join the rest of the expedition!'

I stared. Mr Landells was back again. But I hardly recognised him. He looked so fine in robes instead of his usual clothes! Instead of his hat he wore the biggest whitest turban I had ever seen, and a long coat that sparkled in the sun. But he still had his hip flask attached to his belt. As I watched, he swung his leg over Landa's hump and signalled to him to rise.

'Hut, hut, hut!' he cried, striking Landa with his whip to make him go faster. I strode after him, the strange weight of my pack swaying on my back, down the track in the park around the corner and —

And then I stopped. For I had never seen anything like this in all my life!

More humans than I had thought there could ever be in the world! The whole road was lined with them. Some blew noises through strange metal things, and some banged drums and others clapped their hands and yelled.

There were our wagons and horses (*phut* and *phooey!*), yoked to the wagons and pulling with all their might, for these wagons were heavy. More horses were ridden by men, too.

Truly, it was the biggest caravan the world has seen!

But where were our sheep? Where were the women to make the fires and bake the bread? Surely a caravan this big needed women! Where were the children to collect our dung?

Why was it so noisy, too?

And why so many horses, when they had us good strong camels?

I spat. Not at any person in particular. Not even at the horses. Just a general spit at the foolishness of all this noise and bustle . . .

It was all too much to take in.

The horses in front of me began to walk, pulling their wagons or trotting beneath their riders. Oh, the indignity, to have to stare at horses' tails, instead of striding out in front!

Mr Landells signalled to Landa. He began to walk. So did I, stepping along the road with my nose in the air. The crowds stood back and cheered.

So there I was, with my strange load on my back. My world, which had felt so crooked and out of shape, seemed almost right again. I was in a caravan . . .

And now, it seemed, our caravan was on its way at last.

CHAPTER 19

The Camel's Story

Melbourne, 20 August 1860

But although our caravan was big, it was not a very good one. I had hardly got into my stride before one of the wagons broke.

Why did our caravan need big wagons? A caravan just needs tents and carpets, some flour and a pot or two.

Truly, the ways of humans are strange.

We all stopped while the wagon was fixed. I was irritated that I'd had to break my stride, but I hardly deigned to turn my head to see what all the fuss was about.

We started off again. But I was beginning to feel less happy. I didn't like the smell of the horses pulling the wagons. Nor did the horses like the smell of us. They squealed and twitched their tails and tossed their heads. I was so annoyed I broke away, and chased a man who blew a whistle at me. The crowd scattered as I lunged! But just as I was about to pick him up with my strong teeth Dost Mahomet grabbed my rope.

Phut! And *phooey* too!

Two more wagons broke, which led to more yelling and more fuss. And so we stopped again.

But I endured it all without complaining (much).

At last we set off yet again. But now the horses were really spooked, with us camels stalking so close behind them. I snickered to myself and aimed a spitball at the hindquarters of the one nearest to me. It splattered as it hit and the horse reared, its rider almost falling off.

Finally, just as we were leaving the houses and all the yelling humans behind, with a good smell of grass in front of us and even a horizon I could see, a man rode up on a horse and called for us to stop again.

I ignored him, of course. What camel pays attention to a man on a horse? But Mr Landells called out, 'Yes, Mr Burke.'

I chewed my cud and waited, while all around me people yelled and horses shied, and this Mr Burke yelled as he tried to organise it all.

Then finally we were off again. But this time we camels strode along one side of the road — with me leading the pack camels, of course — and all the horses on the other, with Mr Burke riding his horse Billy between the two lines.

Horses! I spit upon them all.

There wasn't time to walk far now, for the sun was sliding down the sky. But at least we travelled far enough to get away from all the houses, though there were still too many for my liking and the road was hard from cart wheels and hooves.

We camped by a small, muddy creek that wound its way between the paddocks. (Paddocks are the way men divide parts of the world and that is all I am going to say. It is too complicated an idea for a young camel like you to understand.)

We camels were put to graze on one side of the road, and the horses with the wagons on the other. But when I headed down to the creek to drink, Dost Mahomet held me back so that the horses could drink first! Oh, the shame of it! The indignity! I spit upon those horses, I do indeed!

But I held my temper. I didn't bite or kick, or even spit, except once at a horse who dared to stare at me too hard. I told myself that horses were weak beings and needed water more than us strong camels, and this was why they had their drink before us.

At last Rajah and the others and I could drink our fill. The water tasted good, too. I couldn't remember when I had last tasted running water that smelt of soil and rock and sunlight, not of a bucket or rain barrel. Then Dost Mahomet and the others gave us some grain — not much, for there was grass, and there were even a few bushes for us to graze on.

I'd already scouted around. The best grass was on the horses' side of the road (*phut* and *phooey!*). So I headed over there, as fast as my hobbles would let me.

Dost Mahomet grinned, as though he had expected exactly that. 'None of that,' he said to me. He grasped my lead rope and led me back to the camels' side. 'Here you are, Bell Sing, back where you belong.'

So I began to eat. Fresh food at last, good grass and leaves! They tasted different from the ones at home. But good. The sky above and the world below, and tomorrow I would walk in a caravan again.

Yes, life was getting back to normal at last.

CHAPTER 20

Dost Mahomet's story

Moonee Ponds (outskirts of Melbourne), 20 August 1860

It was not a good start to the journey. The wagons broke. Men got drunk and fought. Mr Burke fired three of them, and hired four more even before we had left the city that first day. *Ha*, I thought. Men like those would run from the bang of an empty gun.

We had only made it to the outskirts of Melbourne by nightfall, when we had to camp. Esau Khan made a special fire for the four of us, just beyond the tents. After our sunset prayers we had approached the big fire where the other men in the expedition sat, cooking their meat on sticks above the flames. But one of the men yelled something at us — words I didn't understand. It was clear they didn't want us at their fire.

I thought of the way we had all sat together each night on the way to Karachi, even though we were men of different lands and faiths. But this was

Australia. Things were different. *Perhaps*, I thought, *it would be better for us cameleers to have a fire to ourselves. We could cook our own food there, and make sure that it was not pork, and had been killed properly, as Allah requires. We could talk freely without being overheard.*

For already there were things that worried me about this expedition.

I squatted by the fire and took the hunk of salt beef Belooch passed me. Simla sat beside me and nibbled on a small piece of bread.

'What do you think of it all?' Belooch asked us softly.

Esau Khan coughed before he answered. I hoped that now we were away from the city the good clean air would cure him.

'Most of the men are drunk!' he said. 'And how can an expedition have a leader who does not even know not to mix camels and horses? Any child in a caravan can tell you that.' He shook his head. 'I tried to tell Mr Burke, but he yelled at me to go back to my camels.' I glanced at Esau Khan in the firelight. I had seen Mr Burke slash at him with his whip too. But I would not embarrass my friend by saying so.

'The wagons are overloaded, even with the extra three Mr Burke hired before we left,' said Simla. He glanced over at Mr Burke's tent and shook his head. We could see Mr Burke sitting there grandly at his big polished table, a giant candelabra filled with candles that flickered in the evening breeze. 'They even have brushes to flick the dandruff from their coats! What does a caravan need with things like these?'

What caravan has a leader who hasn't even worked out which way to go? I thought. But I didn't say it. I was still afraid the others might decide to leave.

'Think of our wages,' I said quietly. But inside I was thinking: *It is worth anything to be part of an adventure like this.*

CHAPTER 21

Dost Mahomet's Story

Bolinda, 23 August 1860

Simla left our expedition at Bolinda three days later. His face was thin with hunger, for he had had nothing but bread to eat since we left Melbourne, though he had worked as hard as any of us.

Simla had tried to talk to Mr Burke, to ask him to advance him wages to buy a sheep or goat that he might slaughter, so he could eat too. But Mr Burke just waved him away. Even Mr Landells just slapped poor Simla on the shoulder.

'You'll just have to make do, boy,' he said. 'If it's good enough for white men it should be good enough for you.'

It was strange, I thought. Back home old Uncle spat at Hindus, and called them 'fish eaters'. Here, among strangers, Simla was our friend.

So Simla said goodbye to us. Tears ran down his face. He had come so far, with so much hope. Now it had all been for nothing.

I watched him trudge back along the track to Melbourne. It was raining, a sharp gusty rain that spat in our faces and left us shivering.

Now there were only three of us.

CHAPTER 22

The Camel's Story

Travelling north of Bendigo, towards the Murray River, August 1860

It was good to be part of a caravan again, even one with so many (*phut!*) horses, and even with all the rain. Luckily there was so much mud that the horses and the wagons could not keep up with us and travelled behind.

Sometimes Mr Landells yelled at us, especially when he had drunk a lot from his flask. Mr Burke yelled too. Yells are an indignity, no matter who is hurling them at you.

But I was among the grass and trees again, away from the buildings and stinking river, and far away from that swaying sea. There were plenty of delicious shrubs to chew, and plenty of things to see as well — cattle and sheep, which are boring, and towns where we were cheered again, though there weren't even any stalls where I could nose out dates or apples.

But there were interesting animals too, big new ones that hopped on two big back legs, and left strange droppings among the grass. They were scared by such fine animals as us, and kept out of our way.

And now I could smell something more.

Rock and sand ahead of us, a far horizon and winds that blew forever. They were still a long way away. But we were heading there.

It smelt like a land that I might learn to love.

Most days were spent just with our caravan, the grass, the wind, which was how things ought to be. But on other days humans ran out of their buildings and stared and shouted at the sight of such fine camels. At other times we saw humans with dark skin and no hats or turbans on their heads. They didn't live in villages, but strode across their land as confident as camels. Once, a few men and a young boy ran right up and pulled my tail, then stood back laughing as I turned and hollared.

'Bunjip! Bunjip!' the boy yelled.

'Get out of it, you thieving savages,' shouted Mr King. He rode over to the boy and raised his whip.

But Mr Wills rode up on his (*phut!*) horse. He reached into his pocket and smiled, and threw some sparkling things down to the little boy. 'Not a bunjip. These just big sheep. You know — *baa baa*.'

The dark-skinned people stared, then laughed politely, their eyes still wide at the sight of my magnificence.

Ah yes, those days were good, even with the horses.

CHAPTER 23

Dost Mahomet's Story

Travelling north of Bendigo, towards the Murray River, August to September 1860

It was hard work now. Twenty-seven camels to load and unload, and to hobble, and only three of us to do it all. None of the others helped us, except for Mr Landells and Mr Wills, who would help take the camels to water.

The three of us woke before dawn. First we cleansed ourselves and prayed. Then each camel had to be fetched in, for even a hobbled camel can travel far if they smell good eating. Everything had to be packed and loaded. Then at the end of the day it was all unloaded again.

The other men tended the horses and loaded the wagons, put up the tents and lit the fires. Mr Wills took notes and measured the way we'd come. Mr Burke rode his horse and yelled a lot.

Most of the men rode horses or in the wagons. Mr Landells rode a camel. Dr Beckler's horse was busiest, dashing here and there as Dr Beckler shouted that he'd found new plants. Sometimes old Dr Becker rode a camel. I had to make it kneel each time Dr Becker wanted to slide off to collect his lizards or beetles. But mostly he rode in one of the wagons, sketching the country as we went.

Dr Becker's sketches fascinated me, but disturbed me too. Allah forbids us to make images of His creation. Yet I found myself drawn to where Dr Becker sat with his charcoal and his paper, turning the world around us into lines that plodded like camels, or laughed like men.

'You like to try it, ja?' Dr Becker offered me the charcoal. But I stepped back and shook my head.

Yes, it was hard. But the land was rich, with good grass and trees. The stars above us swirled in strange new patterns. There were people of the land, too, which no one had told us about. They had black skins and wore few clothes. At first I thought we had been given guns and knives to help protect the caravan, just as we would have at home, and waited for the black men to steal up to us at night to cut out throats.

But the nights were the most peaceful I had ever known.

I was learning the sounds of the bush now. There was a bird that laughed at dawn, almost as though it were calling the three of us to prayer with a cry of delight in the beauty of Allah's creation. When I heard thuds in the night now, I knew it was what the black men called a wallabi, which was like a small kangaroo. Once I saw thirty or more kangaroos leap across the skyline, almost the colour of the sand.

It was strange, but for the first time I thought of what it might be like to stay here forever, to walk from horizon to horizon.

The land was not paradise. The people were too unfriendly to anyone who was not like themselves. But this was also a land that had not known war. One day we passed a camp of shearers, on their way to work. They slept in the open, with no need of a lookout to keep them safe. Only one had a firearm, and that was to shoot the ducks along the creek. (There were so many at every waterhole that Belooch shot three in the time it takes to breathe three times, and Dr Beckler caught a fish so large it fed ten men, though I refused to taste it.)

There is work here, and good money, I thought, as I trudged beside Bell Sing, for anyone who could walk their caravans across the drylands. This country was so vast that a thousand camels would not be enough to bring supplies to the towns and farms here.

This is a land of plenty, I thought. *It is a land of peace.*

I would go home, of course. My family was there, blood of my blood, and voices of my heart. I longed to have men of Allah about me again, to be one of a hundred voices raised in prayer, to dip my hand once more into the common bowl of rice and goat and eat with men of my own kind. But I would never be sorry I followed Mr Landells to this land, with its white trees like ghosts. *I will tell my grandchildren about this,* I thought. *They will call me 'the old man who left his heart in Australia'.*

CHAPTER 24

The Camel's Story

The Murray River, September 1860

At last I smelt a river — a proper one, the sort that travels a long way and knows its business, that floods at times, filling pools that then dry slowly when the rains stay away.

Finally we reached it and began to walk along the bank. I liked its trees, with large trunks dappled cream and grey and small grey-green leaves, singing of deep roots and branches that loved the sun. I drank the river's scent and thought, *Yes, this is good.*

That first night by the river I dipped my nose in and drank. Ah, young camel, this waterhole may taste sweet. But a river has a story of all the lands it has passed through. Surely this river had the richest story in the world.

I drank deeply, loving the rich scent. For the first time I thought, *If only I were not tethered, not hobbled. If only I could follow this river to find the source of all these scents. If only I were free . . .*

I had never thought anything like that before. I had accepted that it is a camel's fate to walk with men. But I had seen so many new things now. And this caravan felt wrong.

Still, the thought disturbed me. I put it away, in the back part of my mind. But from now on it would wriggle out again. Once you think things, they can never truly be put away.

CHAPTER 25

John King's Story

The Murray River, September 1860

We'd just set up camp by the Murray. Not bad country, except for the pests. The flies crawled in your eyes and up your nose. Your chops were crawling with them as soon as you took them from the fire. The mosquitoes bit through everything except our boots. Even the ants stung, and were big enough to eat out a horse's eyes. They fascinated old Becker, who even admired the country's scentless flowers. But I was used to vermin from India.

We'd seen natives on our way here. There hadn't been any trouble — they were well outnumbered down here in settled country. But I suspected things might be different once we finally reached uncharted lands.

The tents were up, and Burke's table set with its candelabras. I liked that — it lets the whole side down if you let standards slip. I'd got one of the men to fill a bath for me. I was just trimming my beard when I heard yelling. I wiped the soap off and ran to see what was happening.

Mr Burke and Mr Landells stood by one of the wagons.

'What are you saying, Burke?' Mr Landells was red with rage. 'Come on, come out with it!'

'Shut it, Landells. Someone's stolen half the rum and it wasn't the camels!' Mr Burke shouted back. His face was red too and his fists were white with anger.

'Are you accusing me?' yelled Landells.

Of course he is accusing you, I thought. *A horse trader like you probably sold the rum at the last shanty.*

'I'm not accusing anyone! I'm stating facts!' screamed Burke. 'Some of that rum is gone! You are a drunk, and incompetent with it!'

'Me, incompetent? You're not fit to wipe a camel's backside. Where would you be without me, I'd like to know?'

'With sixty gallons of rum untapped, that's where we'd be! And I don't need a drunk like you to teach me my business . . .'

'Your business! Why, you arrogant upstart . . .'

Mr Burke grabbed an axe and marched into the tent. Two seconds later he was out again, pushing a barrel in front of him.

Landells suddenly realised what he was going to do. 'No!' he shouted. 'Burke, you're crazy! The camels need that rum!'

'Crazy, am I?' Burke lifted up the axe and brought it down on the barrel. I caught the smell of rum even from where I was standing.

Landells stood there staring. For a moment I thought he was going to strike Burke. Suddenly he saw me, in the shadows of the trees. 'He's mad,' he said. 'Mad and a fool. And anyone who follows him is a fool too. I'm leaving in the morning. And if you have any sense you'll quit too.'

I watched him stride back into the camp.

Landells wrote up his resignation that night. But he withdrew it — scared, I think, that he might not get his pay.

Gossip flew around the expedition. Landells had cursed Burke. Landells had said Burke hated Wills — or Beckler — or me — and planned to dismiss us all. No one knew the truth, yet one thing was plain. We had not even started our exploration. But the hatred between our two leaders was already breaking the expedition apart.

By the time we reached Swan Hill township I really began to worry.

CHAPTER 26

Dost Mahomet's Story

Swan Hill, 6 September 1860

Every traveller knows the joy of a river after days of dry tramping — the soft sounds of water, the hush of trees and the song of birds above. There was a generosity about a river flowing through drylands. Every river I had known seemed to whisper, *Rest here, after the harshness of the world around.*

I liked the township of Swan Hill too. The river there flowed slowly and calmly. Big trees hung above it, their shadows flickering as the water glinted in the sun. A punt carried people and horses from one side to the other.

Another river joined the Murray at this point, so that the waters spread into a giant lagoon. A wave of swans and water birds surged into the sky with a *crack* as we approached — so many that it was easy to shoot all you wanted in the time it takes to draw a breath. There were fish too, almost as big as a man, with firm sweet flesh. The men roasted them on the coals of the fire. I had never eaten fish before. I had a sudden memory of old Uncle, calling a hated neighbour a 'fish eater'. A true man eats meat, not fish. So I ate it reluctantly. The taste was good, but it was soft, an old man's food. After I had eaten it my teeth felt like they still needed something to chew.

But you didn't have to travel far from the river for the country to become dry, with small, twisted, dark trees with many trunks growing out of reddish sand.

The people at Swan Hill welcomed us warmly, yelling and cheering as we arrived. They wandered through the camp, staring at the camels. They stared at Belooch and Esau Khan and me as well, as though they weren't sure which was the strangest sight. But I was growing used to being stared at by now.

The crowds meant more work for us, as we had to make sure that no one harmed the camels — and that the camels didn't try to gum the townsfolk either. But it was good to see the wonder on the children's faces.

The cough that Esau Khan developed in Melbourne had not got better as we walked. Sometimes now when he coughed there were spots of blood on his lips. At night he grew hot with fever. Belooch and I did as much as we could, to let him rest. But it was impossible for the two of us to get the camels loaded as quickly as Mr Burke wanted. Mr Burke was even touchier these days. Mr Burke had already fired several men for drunkenness.

But now he and Mr Landells were like dogs who snarl at each other before a fight.

One night Esau Khan's coughing was especially loud.

'What's that noise?' Mr Burke stomped over to our fire. 'You!' he cried.

Esau Khan rose shakily to his feet. His face shone with the sweat of his fever. 'Sahib?'

'I've been watching you laze about while the others work — don't think I haven't noticed. You're sacked.'

Esau Khan stared at him. 'I am sorry, sahib. I do not understand.'

'You're finished,' shouted Mr Burke, as though yelling louder would help Esau Khan understand the English words. 'Off with you, tomorrow. Back to Melbourne. Understandee?'

'Sahib,' I broke in, speaking as calmly as I could, 'our brother here is sick. But he will be well again. We can do his work while he gets better.'

Mr Burke's face grew red. 'You'll be off too if you can't hold your tongue! Sick or lazy, it's all one to me. I won't have a man who can't pull his weight.'

What sort of leader is this? I thought. What sort of man shows no charity to one who is ill?

Esau Khan's face was white in the firelight. I said urgently, 'Sahib, he will need money to get back to Melbourne. Can he have his wages, please? He will need his fare back home too.'

Mr Burke was already striding away. 'Wages? You'll get wages when the expedition's over, not before.'

'But his fare, sahib?' I urged, trying to look polite, and not as if I wanted to slip a dagger in his side. (I would have gladly, but it would have been no help to Esau Khan.) 'Mr Landells promised our fares back home would be paid.'

'Then get Landells to give you the money!' he barked, storming off.

That night Belooch and I went from man to man around the camp, trying to collect a few coins for Esau Khan. Dr Beckler gave us the most, and a few others like Mr Wills and Dr Becker gave us money too.

It would not be enough to pay his fare back home. But at least he would make it to Melbourne without starving.

'Find the expedition's organisers,' I urged him. 'The Royal Society, it is called. They will pay your wages, and your fare home too.'

Esau Khan nodded. His hands trembled as he lifted his bundle of blankets and clothes. But my heart felt as heavy as a bag of flour. None of us knew how to find this Royal Society. We had never even met them back in Melbourne. And Esau Khan was sick, in a strange land, with no one to care for him.

But what could any of us do?

CHAPTER 27

Dost Mahomet's Story

Balranald to Gobanna, September 1860

Now there were only two of us.

Each morning we had to get up long before the others, to fetch the camels. At night, while others rested, we had to hobble them. It was lonely, with just the two of us by our fire.

We laid our prayer mats on the red dirt, trying to imagine we heard the voices of our kinsmen as we chanted.

I had never realised how lonely it can be surrounded by other people, Unbelievers who treated us like their wagons, to use and throw away if we were broken.

Sometimes we smiled, sitting in the darkness as the ferenghis slapped at the mosquitoes. There were no mosquitoes around our fire. We threw camel droppings onto our flames, which kept the mosquitoes away.

The camels meant hard work. But they smelt of home too. Sometimes I shut my eyes as we walked next to them, listening to the soft clomp of their feet, smelling the sweet camel breath, imagining my kinsmen walked beside me. But then one of the men would yell, and I would open my eyes to the Australian plains.

Now that Esau Khan had left, Mr Landells helped us load and unload — partly, I think, to keep away from Mr Burke, for the two still snarled at each other like dogs.

Sometimes Mr Wills helped too, and even Mr King. I had thought Mr King was a man who preferred to give orders than work. Loading camels is a skill — if you don't balance the load the camel can fall, and break a leg. Both Mr Wills and Mr King learnt quickly and worked hard. But they rarely helped us when Mr Landells was there, for they were loyal to Mr Burke.

At Balranald there was a punt, which we used to cross the Murrumbidgee River. The river was lined with shady trees. But the town was small and flat and shabby, and the country was flat too. Low silvery bushes gleamed in the coarse red sand, interspersed with patches of little twisted dark trees.

We camped on the flat in front of the Balranald Hotel.

Belooch and I were unloading the camels when we heard yelling. I glanced at Belooch. He shrugged. 'Some of the men are drunk again.'

I shook my head. 'That is Mr Burke's voice.'

The right answer to a fool's yell is silence. But Mr Burke's quarrels might involve us too. We hurried through our work, then ran into the centre of the camp.

'Liar!' It was Ferguson, the foreman. He waved a rifle at Mr Burke. 'Come on, you coward! Stone the flaming crows! Think you can cheat us, eh? Defend yourself!'

'I won't fight a duel with the likes of you!' screamed Mr Burke.

The whole camp was watching. I made my way quietly over to Dr Becker. 'Sahib, what is happening?'

Dr Becker looked grim. 'Ach, more foolishness. Herr Burke has decided he will sack some men. At first he said that the Expedition Committee ordered it. Now he admits that it is to save money only. Herr Burke has spent too much hiring wagons. He offered to keep the men but pay them less. Now Herr Ferguson wants to fight a duel!'

Suddenly Mr Burke turned his back and marched away. *That is the way to do it*, I thought. *Walk away and let one of your men cut your enemy's throat in the night.*

But the talk of wages worried me. I had thought that Mr Burke's purse was endless. We carried firewood instead of gathering it; we carried salt meat instead of keeping sheep or goats to eat the grass as we went.

What of the money he owed me?

Had Nur been right all along? Was I mad to trust a ferenghi, especially one like Mr Burke?

I could leave now, I thought. *Find work caring for the camels we had left in Melbourne, perhaps, to earn my fare back home. Leave the expedition . . .*

My skin felt cold although the night was warm. For the first time I had to admit I was not here just for the money. Yes, I would fight to get what I was owed. But I would never leave the expedition now.

* * *

But no one's throat was cut that night. Instead Mr Burke ordered stores unloaded from the wagons — food and tools.

'Idiocy!' growled old Dr Becker. He was carrying his specimen jar, already filled with dark brown beetles, with his sketchbook under his arm. 'Where does he think we're going to find food where we're going, hmmm? He even leaves the lime juice!'

He saw I didn't understand. 'Lime juice stops scurvy — your teeth fall out, you swell up and you die. Ach, you ask Dr Beckler. He will tell you about scurvy! If your teeth fall out in the desert, young man, if you die of scurvy, you will know who to thank!'

He stomped off, to look for more beetles perhaps, or to sketch the desert. And I went to water the camels.

We left Balranald in the cool of the morning, soon after the dawn prayer. The ground was soft under the camels' feet now. The red sand seeped into our clothes and eyes and mouths. The horses strained as they tried to pull the wagons. My heart ached for the poor animals.

Why, I thought, *does Mr Burke need to take so much? The bath? The shiny table?*

But even though the loads were less now, day after day the wagon wheels sank into the sand. Every man was needed to shovel them free. At times every horse was harnessed to just one wagon, to try to get it unbogged.

But the camels walked undisturbed. They were still only lightly loaded, for Mr Landells said they must keep up their strength for when we reached the proper desert, and the horses and wagons could go no further. Nor did the lack of water worry the camels, for they fed off the fat stored in their humps. Their wide feet slapped against the sand as they swayed towards the horizon.

Perhaps, I thought, *all will be well.*

CHAPTER 28

Dost Mahomet's story

Gobanna Bush camp, 36 miles from the Darling River, 8 September 1860

'Look at them! Sehr interessent, hmmm?' cried old Dr Becker.

I stared at the snakes in the bottle. There were three of them, one long and brown and the other two small with bands across them. Dr Beckler and Dr Becker grew excited at the strangest things.

'Very good, sahib,' I said politely.

Mr Wills had said this would be our last camp before the Darling River. I was looking forward to the river, to be able to cleanse myself properly before my prayers. Suddenly I heard the clanging of the gong, calling the camp together.

I left Dr Becker carefully stowing his bottle in one of the chests, and ran to see what was happening.

Mr Burke stood in front of his tent. His big table was set, as always, with his fine silver and his candelabra. He waited till we were gathered. He looked hot and red. Had he been arguing with Mr Landells again?

You stupid man, I thought. And Mr Landells was a fool as well. Why did not Mr Landells have Burke killed, and take his place, instead of all this bickering?

'Right, listen up!' The men fell silent. 'There are going to be changes. We're leaving the wagons here — the going is too rough for them.'

'Ja. Exactly,' muttered Dr Becker. He and young Dr Beckler had come up beside me.

'From now on each of you is only allowed thirty pounds — equipment, clothes, blankets.'

'Apart from our specimens . . .' began Dr Beckler. 'And the scientific instruments . . .'

Mr Burke grinned. He knew that old Dr Becker and young Dr Beckler sided with Mr Landells. 'Gentlemen, from this time you have to give up your scientific investigations. You'll work like the rest of the men. You'll help load the camels and horses, and then you'll walk. Each and every one of us will walk our twenty miles each day.'

'Impossible!' cried old Dr Becker. 'The whole point of this expedition is to study the new country!'

Mr Burke gave that grin again. 'If you don't like it, Becker, then you can go back home. But you will walk.'

He turned and marched into his tent.

The men stood stunned. Even Mr King looked shocked. 'He can't expect us to walk like a bunch of convicts.'

'Oh yes he does,' said Mr Landells.

I said nothing. What had I to say? Belooch and I were dust under Mr Burke's feet.

That afternoon I helped Dr Becker sort out what he would take, then showed him how to help load a camel. But I could see that the old man would never manage to do it properly.

'It is good that Herr Docktor Beckler and I sent specimens off at Balranald!' Dr Becker shook his grey head. He was nearly crying. 'We have been on the road a month! Most of the expedition's money spent already! And for what? Nothing! Ach, it is insane,' he muttered. 'This is a Royal Society expedition! We are supposed to be men of science, learning about this land. And now this dummkopf makes me throw away my specimens, and work loading the camels and the horses.'

I put my hand on the old man's arm before Bell Sing could gum him. 'Stand back, sahib.'

'Why? Is he savage?'

'No, sahib. But he does not like being loaded.' I gazed at the amount of luggage that had been left for the camels to carry. Even Mr Burke could not expect the smaller camels to carry all that!

I ran to Mr Landells, who was sorting out what luggage he would leave behind. 'Sahib, the loads are too heavy.'

Mr Landells frowned. 'What are you talking about, man?'

'Mr Burke says we must put heavy loads even on the smaller camels, sahib.'

'Burke? What does he think he's doing? The camels are *my* responsibility, not his!'

I ran after him as he charged up to Mr Burke. 'Burke, what in the devil's name are you thinking of? The camels need to keep up their strength for the desert! It's insane to work them to exhaustion now!'

'A pox on your camels, Landells, and you too!' bellowed Mr Burke, looking as if he would hit Mr Landells. 'If I say we leave the wagons here and let the camels carry all the stores, then that's what is going to happen!'

'What do you know of camels? What do you know of anything, you stupid little man?'

'I am the leader of this expedition, that's one thing I know! And if you don't like it you can take your miserable hide back to Melbourne.'

'And what would happen to you then? Your camels would die of exhaustion out there in the desert, and then you'd die too, the lot of you, and crows would pick your bones. You need me, you fool . . .'

Mr Burke's boots almost danced with rage on the hard ground. 'Drunkard!'

'Madman!' Mr Landells shouted back.

But Mr Burke won the battle. I loaded the camels, as he instructed, while Mr Landells marched off swearing.

I had worked with camels all my life, just as my father had in his caravan. We had never lost a camel in all that time. But now, I knew, the riding camels and the smaller beasts would stumble under the great weight, bruising themselves or breaking a leg.

It was not right. But again, there was nothing I could do.

CHAPTER 29

The Camel's Story

Gobanna, September 1860

I had been enjoying myself, watching the world pass by as we plodded across the good red sand, even if I had to keep waiting for the men to unbog the wagons. Even though there was not much grass, the bushes had a fine, salty taste that I particularly enjoyed. They took some chewing, but made delicious cud when I regurgitated them. (Grass is good on the way down but tastes of nothing much after you've chewed it again an hour or two later. But the flavour of saltbush lingers.)

And then one morning it all changed.

Ah, what a weight was loaded onto my back! I had never carried such a load before!

Oh, the strain of it! I moaned and Rajah groaned as well. It was even worse for the riding camels, for they had not been trained to carry a load. Poor Bunjib screamed as she stumbled under the weight. But I did not try to gum Dost Mahomet, or even kick at him.

I knew whose fault it was.

I waited till Mr Burke rode past me on his horse, Billy, yelling as he always did and checking that things were as he wanted.

I waited till he was right in front of me. And then I spat.

It was the best spitball I think I have ever produced. A good big ball of cud, bushes and some tree leaves and a little tussock grass, all chewed and then digested a bit then chewed again. It got him on his cheek.

'Ow!' screamed Mr Burke. He glared at me. I stared back, imperturbable.

He grabbed his whip, then lashed out and caught me on the leg. I roared in pain, and at the indignity too. I would have gummed him, but by the time I'd thought of it he'd ridden off.

From then on Mr Burke glared whenever he passed me — but always from a good distance in case I spat at him again. As for me, I made sure I bawled as loudly as I could whenever his Billy got in front. My noise startled Billy, and every time he skittered and shied, and every time Mr Burke swore.

Ha! I spit upon him. I spit upon his silly horse as well. If he had not angered me things might have been different. If he had known how to apologise to a camel, and to others, like Dost Mahomet or any sensible man, I might have forgiven him . . .

Ah, young one. It was long ago. But the indignity still rankles.

I grew used to the big load soon enough. But the smaller camels never got used to the weight. Something snapped in Bunjib's shoulder, and she limped so badly she slowed us all up.

Now that all the riding camels carried packs, the men all had to walk — all except Mr Burke up on his Billy. And oh, the fuss they made of it! You would have thought they had no feet!

If they had ever seen a proper caravan, I thought, as I munched a few potatoes Dost Mahomet brought me — strange things, but not too bad — *they would have known that it is right for men to walk beside camels. For a caravan cannot go faster than a camel, so why not walk alongside us?*

Even though we still followed a road of sorts, at last the ground was softer and drier under my feet. By now I had learnt a lot about the smells of this new land, learnt to watch the way the clouds skidded across the sky, to sense where the hot winds came from, and understand the scent of water.

One day, I said to myself as I swayed along under my load, I will know this land as well as I know the taste of my own cud. I will own it, just as my mother did the mountain trails.

Now another river, the Darling, twisted its way through the trees. It was a good river, the sort where the water flows and stays sweet, with just the right amount of salt.

Long-legged birds poked about the muddy shores. Belooch waved his gun in the air at the sight, and the birds leapt for the sky, their wings stretched out like clouds. There was a *bang*. One of the birds dropped to the earth, and Belooch ran to grab it.

Ah, it was good camping by that river. Sometimes I wish we had a river like that here. There were large, shady trees with pale mottled trunks that sheltered you from the sun as the days grew hotter. Small blue birds like the jewels in a lady's bangle darted across the water. The strange big animals with long fat tails — which I had learnt were called kangaroos — thumped away as we disturbed them in the shade of the trees.

One evening a flock of tiny green and yellow birds arrived, chirruping and zizzing, to drink at our pool of water and fuss among the grasses. I had never seen so many birds in one place before! Then suddenly the flock took to the air as one, and in a flash they were all gone.

I was happy. There was time to eat and digest, and ponder the mysteries of the universe, such as why a cud tastes more and more different the longer you chew it.

That was before they made me swim the river . . .

CHAPTER 30

John King's Story

Kinchega, on the Darling River, 14 October 1860

I'll never forget that first day's walk. There we all were, trudging through the red dust like a mob of sepoys.

Truth to tell, I enjoyed it, though most of the men complained, and poor old Becker looked like he was going to faint in the heat of the afternoon. But I had to hand it to the old boy — he gritted his teeth and kept on going.

No, it was good to feel my body hard and fit again. Who would have thought I'd be striding alongside the camels like this, after so many months of illness?

It was good to see the Darling at last too. This river had none of the soft brown fullness of rivers at home, with their verdant fields and cows grazing at the edges. But it was beautiful in its own way — a way I was only just starting to become aware of.

It had seemed such a barren land out here at first, the heat and the dryness and the flies.

But sometimes — when the air softened at sunset, perhaps — I saw this land in another way. The enormous distances were fearsome, but exhilarating as well. It excited me to think that our small band was going to conquer it, forge a path for others to follow, even the telegraph and the railways.

At times the sheer size of our endeavour filled me with such delight I could have broken out in song — to the amusement of the other men, I was sure! But at other times . . .

There are things a man shouldn't say about his leader. That is the army way — you never question orders, you just obey. To do otherwise results in chaos, letting the side down.

But to be honest, Mr Burke had worried me the day we first set out, when he lost his temper and fired those first men, and hired others on a whim. I was even more concerned now.

It was as though he was deliberately pushing us to breaking point, to force some of us to resign to save money, for I heard him tell Landells he had overspent already by hiring the three extra wagons.

The arguments with Landells worried me, too. Oh, it was Landells's fault much of the time. But it is a leader's job to keep things in line.

Here we were, still far from the edge of unknown country. Our real work hadn't even started, and already much of our stores and equipment had been left behind, most of the money spent, and there were feuds among the ranks.

I should not have been thinking these things, I knew. But it was impossible not to.

Things between Burke and Landells came to a head that last night by the Darling River. I had been trimming my beard — for even in the bush it is important to keep up appearances. I came out of my tent to find Burke and Landells screaming at each other on the riverbank.

'The camels need a punt to get across, you fool!' shouted Landells.

'Punts cost money. They can swim like the horses.'

'Heaven give me strength,' yelled Landells. 'They're camels, not bloody fish! They're desert animals!'

'You will do as I order you, or else!' Burke was shrieking now. His face was deep red, all control quite lost.

'Or else what, you stupid man?'

I caught my breath as I always did at Landells's insults. Never, in my wildest moments, had I dreamt of calling a commanding officer stupid.

Mr Burke grinned suddenly. 'Or else I will put someone else in command of the camels.' Mr Burke raised his voice again. 'Mr Wills, to me! Now!'

Landells stared. 'Wills? You can't put young Wills in my place!'

'He knows to do as he's told! Wills, you're the new second in command.' Burke grinned. 'We're the Burke and Wills Expedition now, eh? King!'

He'd seen me watching. 'Yes, sir?'

'"Sir"! That's how you speak to your leader, Landells! King, you're in charge of the camels from now on.'

I was dumbfounded. But all I said was, 'Yes, sir.'

'What do you think you're doing?' screamed Mr Landells. 'King knows as much about camels as I know about knitting!'

Mr Burke turned to me. 'Well, Mr King, if I order you to swim the camels acoss the river will you do it?'

'Yes, sir. Of course.'

'There's no "of course" about it!' cried Landells. 'You can't treat a camel like a horse! They won't stand for it!'

Burke shrugged. 'Get on with it,' he said to me shortly.

Landells flung his hat onto the ground. 'That's it. I resign.'

Burke shrugged. 'As you like,' he said.

I saw him smile as he walked away.

I went back to my tent to finish dressing, confused and, I must admit, worried. Would the sepoys know how to get the camels to swim across a river? I could only hope they did, for I did not.

I had great respect for Wills — a hard worker, meticulous, careful and invariably good tempered no matter what we faced. But he simply didn't have Landells's experience.

But my old military instincts were still alive within me. Mr Burke was my commander. It was my duty to follow him, no matter what his orders. And when it came down to it, what else can a man do, except his duty?

And now I had to work out how to get the camels across a river.

CHAPTER 31

The Camel's Story

Darling River, October 1860

Have you ever seen a river, young camel? It is wet. Wetness is good when you stick your nose in it and drink. But not when humans float across on wooden things and drag you after them.

Yes, it is true! Right into the water! Rajah was dragged into the river first, up to his knees, then deeper, deeper, till suddenly he floundered in the water!

Ah, but he was a big fine camel. I watched him struggle in the water, with the humans pulling at him. And at last he clambered up onto the other side.

And then it was my turn. Ah, the feeling when my feet were washed away from solid ground! The terror as I splashed around! But yes, I made it too!

Impossible you say? *Phut! Gurgle!* That shows how little you know! Every one of us camels made it across the river: Golah Sing, Rowa, Nero, Rangee, Shadow . . . *Phut! Gurgle!* But it is something I will never do again!

CHAPTER 32

Dost Mahomet's story

Menindie, 16 October 1860

We followed the Darling River to Menindie. It should have been easy walking by the water. But the camels staggered under their heavy packs along the sandy soil. We had lost two already, so badly injured by their heavy loads they had to stay behind. The horses strained and sweated, for they were overloaded too.

The mail coach passed us as we walked, the wheels thundering dust along the track.

'Ach,' muttered old Dr Becker. His face was flushed. 'The mail coach, it takes a week to get to Menindie from Melbourne. Two months it has taken us! We could have sent the stores by paddle steamer from Adelaide, instead of breaking the backs of the poor animals. We could all have sailed right up here to Menindie. In one week all would have been here! But nein, nein. We have to walk from town to town! And now summer it is coming, and the money has run out . . .'

'The money, sahib?' When Dr Becker was exhausted it was hard to understand his words. Dr Becker glanced at me from under the brim of his hat.

'The cheques, they have been bouncing.' He saw I didn't understand. 'Mr Burke pays for things with paper called cheques, for the bank to pay the money. But Mr Burke has used up all the money in the bank.' His voice grew faint. For a moment I thought he was going to fall. I put my shoulder under his arm. Young Dr Beckler saw that the old man was weak, and ran to his other side.

'Ach,' whispered Dr Becker. 'You are good boys. It is right that you should know . . .'

'My wages will be paid when the expedition is over,' I said. 'That is what Mr Landells promised.'

Dr Becker shook his head wearily. 'Perhaps the committee will give more money to the expedition. Perhaps.'

At last we saw the township of Menindie in the distance. It was tiny — huts made of wood and cloth. But it had a baker's shop, and what the men called a pub, a place where alcohol was sold.

Mr Burke stayed there, and Mr Wills and Mr King. The rest of us camped by the river.

Suddenly there was a commotion at the other fire, where most of the men sat.

Belooch swallowed his mouthful of salt beef. 'Something has happened.'

A figure broke from the other group, and limped over to us. It was old Dr Becker. 'Mr Burke, he has made one of his decisions,' he said. He lowered himself slowly onto the ground beside us. 'No one has told you, hmmm?

'The people here who know the country have told Mr Burke it is insane to go north now, with summer coming. They say we should be staying here till the rain comes when it is cool, and there is grass and water.

'But Mr Burke says no. Dummkopf! Why can he never do things that are right, hmmm? He says now that most of the men will stay here. He will take a small group, strong men only, and the strongest of the animals, north to the Cooper River. Then a few of them will go the rest of the way to find a way to the north.'

I felt a hand take my heart and squeeze. 'Who will stay here?' I whispered. Surely it wasn't my destiny to come so far, just to be left at Menindie?

Dr Becker shrugged. 'He does not say yet. He is afraid, I think, that Mr Stuart will set out from Adelaide, and cross the land before him. All the beetles I have discovered, all the new surveys we have done, it is nothing to Mr Burke. He must be first to reach the coast or he is dust.'

I was silent. It seemed right to me. We must be the first!

Surely, I thought, *Mr Burke must take me and Belooch. He needs us for the camels!*

'Ach, it is madness!' Dr Becker was saying. 'Dr Beckler is resigning. Work he cannot, with a man like that! So now we will have no doctor in our party! Madness.'

I hardly heard him. All I could think was: *Let Mr Burke choose me.*

Mr Burke rang his gong next morning. Much had been left behind, but not his gong. He read out the list of names.

Ten camels were to stay at Menindie. Sixteen were to go north . . . Landa, Gotch, Beer, Rajah, Rowa, Bell Sing . . .

Eight men were to stay. Eight were to go north. Mr Burke, Mr Wills, Mr Grey, Mr King . . .

And me.

Belooch's eyes narrowed with anger. 'What son of a pig will not take the men who know the camels best? I am the best shot, too.'

I said nothing. It was true.

'You and I should go back to Melbourne,' said Belooch furiously. 'Dr Beckler will take us on the paddle steamer with him. He is a good man. He will make sure the expedition people down in Melbourne pay us what we're owed. My friend, you must not follow Mr Burke. You cannot let a madman lead you in the desert.'

'And the camels?'

'Let the ferenghis care for their own camels!'

I watched the ducks fly up across the river. Did the ducks know what lay north? I wondered.

Was Mr Burke a madman?

I did not admire Mr Burke. But I had seen a fire in his eyes that I could share.

I wanted to go north. I wanted men to say in a hundred years 'Dost Mahomet walked this way'.

'I am going,' I said quietly. 'We have come too far to go back now.'

I waited for Belooch to argue. But he didn't. He stared at me. At last he said, 'Then I will stay here. To care for the camels. To wait for you. To help bring the stores, when money comes to pay for them. If I stay

I can help get supplies to you. Old Dr Becker is staying too.' He smiled at me suddenly, his teeth white in his beard. 'Perhaps we are all crazy?'

'Perhaps,' I said.

Belooch and I chose a tree along the river a little way from the camp for our prayers. We could wash ourselves there in the good running water, and spread our mats and pray without the stares of the other men. Sometimes they made rude comments.

The sun had set now, though the sky still had a haze of pink along the skyline. The first star shone out where the sky pooled darker overhead. We sat back, in that peace that comes after prayer, enjoying the silence after the bustle of the camp and the few moments of stillness before we began work again.

And I was going north. For now that was all that mattered.

CHAPTER 33

The Camel's Story

Menindie, then on towards Cooper's Creek, 19 October 1860

When our caravan set off again it was far from the biggest caravan in the world. But Rajah and I still walked together. And the land was flat and good, with plenty of food for me to nibble on. I could smell that rain had passed this way not long ago. For the first time I began to think that possibly this fiery man might know a little, to have brought us to such good grass just after rain.

But then we began to walk over rocky hills, where the horses' hooves struck sparks from the rock. They panted in the heat and their coats gleamed with sweat — such a waste of good moisture!

Ha! I thought. *No horse pulling a wagon could have come this far.*

Day after day we walked — into grassland now. I kept waiting for Mr Burke to signal us to stop, like any good head man would. Then we and the horses could eat our fill put on some fat again, to make up for the weight we'd lost with all this travelling. This grass would soon dry up, and I could smell no more rain on the horizon. We needed to eat lots while we could!

But Mr Burke just kept us walking. No longer did I think he knew what he was doing. We plodded on from the moment the sun came up until the shadows lengthened in the evening.

I smelt the wind. It brought the scent of rain, and grass to come — but not in the direction we were travelling. We should face the wind and find its secrets! *If only I were free*, I thought again, *not tethered in a caravan, bound to foolish men like Mr Burke. If only I could follow the wind instead of being forced to go where the foolish led . . .*

It was the second time I had thought that, what it would be like to be free. But it was not the last.

We came to a creek of sand, where the men had to dig until water at last seeped through. The horses (*phut!*) drank nearly all of it, so we camels only had a mouthful each. But that was life. We could survive on far less water than they could.

We trudged past scattered misshapen trees and over sandhills. We walked across fine flats of grass but didn't even pause to browse. We drank at waterholes, some of them good ones, with cool water, that smelt like they were never dry.

This is a good land, I thought, *spoilt only by the humans and their* (phooey!) *horses*.

For the first time I didn't miss my home. This was starting to become my land now. I was learning as we walked, learning to feel the land with my broad feet, learning its smells, learning to sense the hint of moisture in the breeze upon my skin.

We came to a river, with mud flats that stank and made it hard to get to the water. There were high sandhills along its banks, and dry bushes that tasted good. We walked through strange woodlands of many-trunked, crooked trees, with so many fallen branches it was hard to find a place to put my feet. The horses found it even harder going.

But soon the ground was dust instead of grass. There were only tussocks now, and too far apart for us to eat much. My feet were happy, even if my stomach missed the grass, At least there were still salty-tasting bushes around.

The days were growing hotter, and longer too.

At last I smelt water, a day or two ahead. If horses spoke camel I might have told them, for I could see that they were thin and thirsty, and suffering from the loads they carried, while we camels still strode ahead. But horses don't speak camel, so they had to wait till they could smell it too. Oh, how they strained and pulled to reach it, while we camels swayed along, our dignity intact as always!

Horses! *Phut!* And *phooey* too!

CHAPTER 34

John King's Story

Near Cooper's Creek, 18 November 1860

Burke had hired a local Menindie man, William Wright, to take us two hundred miles north as far as Torowotto Swamp. There Burke made Wright third in command, and sent him back to take charge of the men and camels left at Menindie. Wright would wait there for money from Melbourne to buy supplies, and bring them up to us at Cooper's Creek.

I will never forget that morning at Torowotto. The sun blazed as it rose beyond the flat horizon. Burke's whiskers were stained with dust. 'Well,' he said. 'I give you all a choice. You know what we face now. You may go back with Wright here, and none will think the worse of you. Or you can come with me, into the unknown.'

I had my doubts of him before. But not now. At this moment Burke was truly great. For the first time I knew that no matter what we would face Burke would get us to the coast. The land would try to beat us. But we would win.

We cheered him then. A big black crowd of crows rose squawking at our noise.

When Wright walked back that morning there was not one of us who chose to go with him.

And so we walked through the dun-coloured plains, across the scattered tussocks, up towards the Cooper, towards the lands that no white man had seen.

The dust got into everything. In our food at night, our water in the morning. It seeped up our nostrils and made our eyes weep, and sucked the moisture from our lips so they cracked and swelled. At times I even envied the sepoy his turban. He wrapped it round his face, so he didn't breathe in dust. The sky was so blue it looked unreal, and the only relief from its blueness was the red haze. I couldn't remember when I'd last seen a cloud.

At night we heard the dingoes howl about our camp. It was a lonely sound, reminding us how far we were from all that is civilised. Even the dogs in this country didn't bark properly. It was strange, but exciting too, to think that we were on the edge of unknown country. Soon we'd be at Cooper's Creek. And after that Burke, Grey, Wills and I would venture forth where no white man had gone before. The sheer hugeness of what we were attempting thrilled me.

Sometimes I looked at the land around us and thought of the roads and railways that would eventually follow us, tethering this land to the Empire. It was wild land now. But soon we would control it, too. *Yes*, I thought. *Finding new lands, expanding the Empire — how could soldiering compare to this?*

Yet one night I woke with the horrors, the sweat dripping off me. I'd dreamt I was back in India, in the Mutiny. I saw the women's bodies, ripped from throat to sternum . . .

It was strange to wake and find myself in the tent, my air pillow under my head. It was the first time I'd had the nightmare since I left India. Was it because we were finally heading into unknown country? Who knew what the natives would be like there, or what we'd face?

Suddenly I felt responsibility weigh on me like a blanket. No one else in this expedition knew how natives can smile on you one day, then turn on you the next. *Perhaps this is why God spared me back in India*, I thought, *to help protect this great project.* I stepped out and breathed in the still, cool air. Dawn was breaking, a faint pink across the horizon. Even this land looked soft at dawn. No one was about, except for the sepoy, fetching in the camels.

I looked down at my hands. They were shaking. Had I got the fever again? Why in the midst of this quiet had I been dreaming about India, about the blood and death?

Was it a warning? Were there dangers here I hadn't realised? I went to help the sepoy. He was a silent man. He worked hard too.

Of course he knew I had my eye on him and would make sure he toed the line. It was one of the first lessons a white man learnt when he went to the colonies. You must have respect. You must be in control.

Mr Wills had calculated that we would reach Cooper's Creek tomorrow or the next day, where we would set up our second base camp. It had been three months since we left Melbourne. Soon the true adventure would begin.

CHAPTER 35

The Camel's Story

Cooper's Creek, 20 November 1860

At last we reached a stretch of sand and trees. The men all smiled, as though we had reached some important place. I could see the sand had been a river once, and would be a river again. When the waters flowed the river would run high and wide, branching into many channels then flooding across the country. I had grown up with rivers like that, which came as the snow melted then disappeared as the summer's heat dried them up.

This land was hard on the horses and men. But it was like home for me.

Mr Burke signalled to us to follow the dry creekbed. Finally we came to a giant waterhole where the water rippled in the breeze, with boggy land around, and high sandhills and big trees leaning over the water.

I sniffed the air. A flood had been here not long ago, I realised. It had shifted all those branches up onto the sandhills.

I could smell something else as well. This waterhole would vanish when summer came.

The men put up the tents, and Mr Burke's fine table, which Rajah had carried all the way from the last camp. The men gathered wood and lit the fire. We camels nosed about for food, then wandered down to the waterhole.

The horses kept out of our way. The silly beasts had trouble reaching the water through the mud, but later I saw that they had managed it, at one end of the waterhole, while we drank in peace at the other.

Now, if Mr Burke had known how to run a proper caravan, like the head man did back home, we would have settled here in peace to eat the grass and drink the water. But no, as soon as the tents were up some of the men set out again to explore across the sand dunes, riding their horses with bags of food and water too.

Horses! *Phut!* How could they cope in a land like this? Soon the horses came limping back, panting and rolling their eyes and desperate for a drink.

The next time the men rode us camels instead: me, of course, the biggest and strongest of them all, and Jambel, Gotch and Boocha. The four of us plodded along the sand to more waterholes, then up across the sand dunes into open country.

It was dry, and covered in giant ant hills — so dry it seemed that even the ants had formed a caravan of their own and moved away, for there were plenty of ant tracks but no ants to be seen. Far off there were ranges, where I could smell new greenery. There was a smell of smoke, too, from one of the black-skinned people's fires. Their smoke smelt different from the fires of our caravan — the wood was much the same, but they cooked different foods upon it.

I hoped we might head for the hills, for I could smell storm clouds hovering there. But instead we just turned back.

The camp was almost as we'd left it. But three camels were missing — Siva, Nono and Bunjib. They had gone exploring with some other men, and the men had come back without them.

What had happened to them? It does not feel right when camels vanish like the night.

I gazed around the camp. It stank of human droppings. The horses had already eaten the grass, and looked thinner than ever, and despondent. I exchanged a '*Gmmfft*' with Rajah. He had found some interesting bushes the night before, so I followed him. Just as I did, thunder growled from the ranges I had seen the day before.

I hesitated. Rajah and I exchanged looks. Back home the head man would have broken camp, and gone towards the storm. Somewhere rain was falling and good grass growing. But we would see none of it in a caravan like this.

Dingoes howled nearby. I shivered. I could kick a dingo so hard he flew. But a pack of them was another matter.

'*Grnh*,' said Rajah, which meant, *Don't worry. Remember I am here, my friend. Dingoes may attack a lone camel, but not two big ones like us.*

'*Whnngggh*,' I replied. But the dingoes' call had made me thoughtful.

Dingoes were dogs, and dogs obeyed men, just as we camels did. But some dogs were free . . .

Is it possible, I thought, *for a camel to do that too?* Was that what had happened to the missing camels — had they escaped to freedom? I could happily live without men. But live without my companions, without the routine of the caravan? That would be lonely indeed.

I took a bite of salty bush, just as Mr Burke gave one of his yells.

'Rats!' he yelled. 'Rats in the flour! Rats in the sugar!' He held up a chewed bit of candle, which is what men use to make a tiny fire so they can see at night.

And so we moved the next day, to yet another waterhole, with dusty hills nearby where Mr Burke hoped the rats would not find us. But any camel worth his hump could smell that there were rats here too.

CHAPTER 36

Dost Mahomet's Story

Cooper's Creek, 28 November 1860

The work was so hard my body screamed for rest. There were twelve camels left to care for now. I tried to show Mr King and the other men how to load and unload them, and how to give the right commands. But it takes many years to understand a camel properly, and learn to work with them. Already they had let three camels stray on a trip away from camp. And it was still left to me to hobble them all each night, and bring them in each morning. Now feed was getting scarce they wandered further every night.

I was even lonelier than before. Old Uncle's saying was true: Five fingers are brothers, but not equals. It was hard working with Mr King too. He spoke to me with words from one of the languages of India, as though there was just one tongue for all the many peoples the Britishers called 'sepoys'. When I did not understand he just spoke louder.

My father would have slit your throat, I thought. But I was not my father. My father would have left this expedition long ago, with the first doubt about our wages.

Mr King spent most of his time now helping put up a stockade about our camp, to keep the black-skinned men away. It is true they stole things in the night. But we had rifles and they did not, and enough men to keep a lookout in the dark.

It was hard without Belooch. I had not known you could feel so alone with others around you. I wondered whether Belooch felt the same, back in Menindie.

There was no one to talk to now except the camels. Even if I had known more words of their language, the other men would still have ignored me.

There was no one to pray with at the set times of the day. Nor was there clean running water to wash myself, as it is written a man must do before he prays. I used the cloth of my turban to filter the water from the waterhole, for it was soon filthy with the droppings of the horses and the camels.

I tried to keep to the laws of diet as best I could. It was not difficult, for there was so little fresh meat, except a bird one of the men managed to shoot, or sometimes a fish. But they did not share them with me. Instead I ate bread from our supplies of flour and rice, and a small bit of the dried beef left from Melbourne. It was so tough and black now I could not cut it with my knife. At times I longed for a familiar bowl of rice and goat, with the hands of kinsmen scooping the food with me. But no. Instead each man was given his portion once a day. So much flour, or rice, or dried meat, like we were little children who had not learnt how to share. We cooked our own, holding the food close to us, as though we did not trust each other not to snatch it away.

Why didn't Mr Wright come with the stores up from Menindie? *Belooch could get the camels up here,* I thought, *if anyone could.* Had they all died, trying to cross the summer desert, that had been so green for us in spring? Would we starve here at Cooper's Creek?

The heat rose about us, like breath from a bread oven. The grass our animals had eaten on the way up would have shrivelled now.

Frustration ate at me, like the rats nibbling our stores. Here we sat starving, our waterhole growing filthy, the flies breeding in our muck.

Old Uncle had been right, as well as wrong. Some ferenghis washed. But none of them knew how to keep a camp clean, and men and camels healthy.

There were fresh waterholes down the river. There was food for the camels to eat. But we sat here, starving and growing sick. The black-skinned men were strong, while we faded into bones.

Day after day they came, silent as shadows through the white-trunked trees, offering fish they'd caught, and sometimes birds. Mr Burke or the others fired into the air to frighten them away.

Yet they came back, with still more fish.

I did not understand it. Why did they keep trying to give us food? Did the black men want us to help them fight their enemies with our guns?

I would have been glad to help them fight, in exchange for food, for their knowledge of this land. Better than sitting here, as food for flies. But no enemies appeared.

And we grew thinner still.

CHAPTER 37

John King's Story

Cooper's Creek, 15 December 1860

I had been right. I knew it when the first tools were stolen, when the natives began offering us fish. My nightmares came every night now, warning me to beware. Sepoys back there, with murder in their hearts. Black men here, trying to steal our food, our tools, our lives . . .

I'd seen it all before. 'Sahib, sahib,' they would say, back in India, salaaming almost to the ground. Then the next night they'd be sneaking up, wielding their knives.

The natives here were just the same. Time after time they brought their fish to our camp, offering them as gifts. Some of the men would have taken them — they were good big fish, and we were on reduced rations, and hungry.

But I'd have none of it. I ordered the men to let off a revolver if the savages came too close.

Here we were, on the edge of the unknown, and they were lurking, just as they had been in the Mutiny back in India. Waiting till we were asleep, and defenceless. Waiting to attack.

'We must build a stockade,' I said to Mr Burke, and he agreed. Mr Burke didn't trust the natives either. Time after time there'd been things missing from the camp — nails or bread or bits of cloth. Thieving savages, the lot of them.

Most of our men had never even seen a stockade built — had no idea how to sharpen the tops of every pole, to make it impossible for the enemy to climb over them in the night, or how to bury the other end deep enough so that no matter how hard the enemy pushed they couldn't force it over.

The men would be safe inside the stockade. The stores would be safe too, those precious stores we'd need when we returned, victorious. We would only take supplies for about three months. Brahe's men had enough for about the same length of time. Surely by then Wright would have come up from Menindie, with more food and men. A bigger party would help keep the savages at bay.

Mr Burke, Wills, Charley Grey and I would head north tomorrow. At last! This was what we'd come all this way for! Grey was good with horses. I'd be in charge of the camels. Wills would survey our route.

Brahe would be left in charge at Cooper's Creek. He was a good chap. Not educated, or a leader — he'd been a drover when he'd joined the expedition. But all he had to do was obey orders. He would wait at Cooper's Creek Camp for us for three months — plenty of time, said Burke, for us to get to the coast and back. If we weren't back then we'd have headed off on an easier route via one of the Queensland stations. Or we'd be dead.

Privately Wills asked Brahe to stay for four months, not three. Brahe agreed. It made me uncomfortable to hear Wills question Burke's decision. But I too was happier to know Brahe would wait for us a bit longer.

We'd scouted out the land to find the best route as best we could. The time wasn't ideal, I had to admit. There were clear signs that this land received rain in winter but shrivelled in the heat. And we were still waiting for Wright to bring the supplies up from Menindie. But if we didn't make a dash north now, Mr Stuart might beat us to it.

Stuart was an experienced bushman — none of us said it aloud, but we all knew it. We were amateurs compared to him. We had taken months just to reach our starting point.

There was no way of knowing what sort of country lay ahead.

Mr Burke was sure there'd be an inland sea, out of which the northern rivers flowed. Sometimes I saw it in my dreams. Lake King, perhaps. Or we'd name it after Her Majesty, Victoria's Sea . . .

Tomorrow, Burke, Wills, Grey and I would show the world once more what the men of the Empire are made of. I remembered being back at school in Dublin, looking at the faces in our classroom and thinking, *Which of you will leave your bones in some foreign land? Who will be the hero, who the coward? Is the fate of the man printed on a child's face?*

I wondered which of those children had died already, of illness in a foreign field, or by a native's spear. I thought, *Tomorrow Burke and Wills and Grey and I march to our destiny.*

CHAPTER 38

The Camel's Story

Cooper's Creek, 16 December 1860

The hot air shivered above the ground even now in the early morning.

Landa rubbed himself against the tree where we sat, waiting for the cool of evening, when we could look for food. Flies had burrowed into his skin to lay their eggs. Sometimes he snuffled with the pain.

Gotch itched too, though not as badly. The itch comes when you do not have good food. The smaller camels were starting to get really hungry. The stronger you are, the further you can roam at night, even with your hobbles on. And the further you can go, the more food you find.

Rajah and I were still strong now, even though we weren't as fat as we had been when the caravan set out. Our humps had shrivelled on the last part of the journey here. But at least we had water, and shade to lie under, and there were still bushes to eat, if you were strong enough to roam far enough to find them.

Suddenly I saw Dost Mahomet walk towards us through the trees, a lead rope in his hands. Dost Mahomet looked thinner these days too.

Ah, I thought, *we are going to move at last*.

I watched as he loaded Landa up with as much as he had ever carried before, and Boocha and Golah Sing too.

Then Dost Mahomet placed a blanket on me. I sighed as he began to load me up. Didn't he know I needed more fat on me to bear a load comfortably! I muttered at the first bundle, then grimaced at the next one, and the next one too. I was just preparing for a thorough moaning when Mr Burke stomped up.

'What are you doing with that brute?' he barked.

Dost Mahomet stared at him, for Mr Burke often spoke too quickly and too angrily for him to understand.

'What is it?' That was nice Mr Wills. He gave me a piece of bread sometimes. A man of manners, who knew how to respect a camel. A higher compliment I cannot pay.

Mr Burke gestured to Dost Mahomet. 'This fool is loading up Bell Sing. I won't have that animal along.'

Mr Wills stared at him. 'But, sir, Bell Sing's the strongest camel of them all!'

Mr Burke shook his head. 'He's savage and unreliable.'

'Not if he's treated right, sir.'

'Are you saying I don't know how to handle a camel?'

'No, sir. Of course not. But, sir, this dash to the coast may be hard going. We need to take the strongest camels of all. And he's a pack camel. He'll be more sure-footed with a load on his back than a riding camel.'

'Who is the leader here?' Mr Burke's voice was rising in volume.

'You, sir.'

'Thank you. Unload that camel. We'll take Rajah instead.'

I watched as Dost Mahomet loaded Rajah. This did not feel right to me. Why was Mr Burke taking riding camels, not pack camels who could carry a heavy load? Why was he walking into the heat, where I could smell that there was worse heat to come?

I gazed at Mr Burke. He was a silly man. But suddenly I saw something else about him too.

It was the look that Bilhari had had the night he faced a wolf who would have taken the young lambs. It was the look of my mother when she was determined to save our camp from the avalanche.

It was the look of someone who will face danger or even death to do what must be done.

I had never thought of Mr Burke in that way before. I wondered what he was expecting to find, to have that look upon his face. For wherever he was going, whatever he knew he had to face, he was taking my best friend in the world along with him.

If I had never spat at Mr Burke, perhaps he would have taken me too.

I watched as they all left — six of them, with Rajah in the lead.

I didn't say goodbye to Rajah, for that is not the camel way. He was a good camel.

He could have snorted at me in triumph, because he was leading his tiny caravan, while I stayed behind.

But he didn't.

I stood there underneath the trees and watched them walk away. I watched as the heat ripples took them and turned them into shimmers. I watched till they merged into the far horizon and were gone.

I wanted to go too. I wanted to be walking, into that wriggle where the desert met the sky. It should have been me there, alongside Rajah.

The shadows grew shorter about me, but still I watched, even though there was nothing left to see.

CHAPTER 39

Dost Mohamet's Story

Cooper's Creek, 16 December 1860

I watched them go, past the black shadows of the trees, up the bare sandhills, into the hot bright air. Four men who did not know the land, or camels; six riding camels, laden with big packs, and Mr Burke's horse.

And all I could think was, *I should be there.*

We waited.

The days grew hotter and hotter still. The waterhole shrank into the mud. There was hardly enough even for the camels to drink, much less all the horses.

The men finished the stockade. Then they did nothing, except sit and sweat. For the first time I was glad the camel work all fell to me. Men need work and challenge. They did not even fish or hunt, though food grew short.

And Mr Wright still did not come.

CHAPTER 40

The Camel's Story

Cooper's Creek, December 1860 to February 1861

We ate. We drank. We waited. There were only six of us camels now, and four men. All of us were thin and we grew thinner still.

The men's droppings grew all sour and loose, and they had to make them many times a day. The camp smelt of sickness. We camels lost the last fat in our humps, no matter how far afield we scavenged for our food. The flies sucked at the skinny ribs of the horses. The poor beasts' eyes grew watery and red, for horses do not have a second eyelid that they can shut, nor can they shut their nostrils as we camels do, to keep out the dust. At time I even felt sorry for them. But then I reminded myself what worthless animals horses were, and worried myself no longer.

Why didn't our caravan set off again, as other caravans did, and go where there was fresh grass and water? Did these men know nothing about how to live?

Why didn't they ask their camels — me especially — where was the best place to travel to next? I could lead them to lots of grass and water! I could smell it far off on the night air. It tantalised me when the breeze came up at sundown. My stomach rumbled for that grass at night.

Were we waiting for Rajah and the others to return? Then why not follow their tracks across the sand?

It was as though life offered nothing for these men except sitting in the shade or running off a little way to do their business, holding their stomachs with the pain.

The rats found us again. I'd known they would. The men hung all their stores from the branches of the trees, to keep them from being eaten.

The dark-skinned people came again, offering fish. But the men of our caravan would not touch this food, despite their hunger. Strange indeed are the ways of men. But the ways of the ones in our caravan were stranger still.

CHAPTER 41

John King's Story

Cooper's Creek to the Gulf of Carpentaria, December 1860 to April 1861

The journey started well. Privately I'd worried how we'd get across the stony desert Sturt had discovered — a vast plain of tiny, shiny, weather-varnished stones. The glare was so fierce it could have cooked us. The camels limped, their big feet bleeding.

Burke was sure there was a vast lake to the north of us. But what if this stony desert reached almost to the sea instead?

But Burke was right. We soon passed the stones. And at first we found water to camp by almost every night.

The heat was bad, the light so strong it almost blinded us. But I was used to heat. I gloried that my body was strong again, that I could stride across a land like this.

Christmas was a delight. Grey was the first to see trees in the distance on Christmas Eve, shimmering in the heat as the air rose from the dust.

Trees meant water. Burke laughed. 'I'll name the creek after you,' he promised Grey.

White-winged birds flapped away as we drew near, then settled again to peck at tiny seeds in the tussocks among the dirt. Grey's Creek was nearly a river, clean water, with fish in the deep pools. And for once no flies or mosquitoes or even ants — almost another Christmas miracle.

My dreams that night were sweet. *A few weeks like this*, I thought, *and we'll be at the coast.*

Burke hoped Grey's Creek would lead us to the lake. We followed the creek till it turned east. We turned north instead.

Burke called the next river after himself. We wound our way through ranges, carpeted with grass, the trees tall and fine. It was as beautiful a country as I have ever seen.

And then the way grew steeper, and steeper still. Those gentle mountains became our prison. The camels' feet bled into the rocky ridges. The poor beasts sweated under their loads. At each rise we had to pull them, groaning, force them to keep climbing.

We tried going around each high spur, to spare the camels the climb. But each time our way was blocked by cliffs or gullies. Finally Burke said, 'Enough of this. We go in a straight line. Up and over.'

I think I grew to love the camels in those days. I led the big one, Rajah. He groaned with terror up on the high ridges. But he kept on going. All of us, men and camels and Burke's horse Billy. We kept on going.

The camels were staggering when we found a creek at last. We let the camels step into the water. We scooped up water to wash off their blood and sweat.

But Burke had got us through the ranges. We half slid, half walked down a scrubby hill. There was another creek that Burke called after his aunt, Lady Elizabeth Cloncurry.

Was the worst behind us now?

The lake should have been here, beyond the mountains, feeding the streams that led to the sea. It wasn't. But as we plodded onwards none of us spoke the words. It would have been disloyal to our leader to say 'Well, you were wrong.'

Soon we were in more mountains once again. I thought I saw a way between the spurs. I was right. Burke called it 'King's Gap'.

Strange, I thought. (Maybe my mind was wandering even then.) I had dreamt so long of the King River, Lake King, Mount King. And now my name was on something that was not. A gap, a nothing . . .

My gap led us down to a creek. It led us north, and so we followed it.

The country changed. Clouds boiled across the deep blue sky.

We slept to the hum of mosquitoes, in a bath of sweat. The soil was black now. There was greenery for the camels but in return they sank to their knees in mud, a foul stench and sticky.

More clouds coiled above us. Rain would have been a blessing a few months ago. Now it was a curse, a grey flood that attacked us from the sky. No lake, but swamps instead. We waded through water to our waists. Leeches fastening on us, not realising we had little blood to share. We'd already been far longer than we expected. Wc were on half rations now, trying to make our poor food last. Birds rose in clouds of grey and pink, screaming at us, not in fear but anger, as we intruded in their world.

Each day Wills announced the date. It kept us sane. It tethered us to the real world, the world of men and orders we had left behind. We had camped on a small rise (a flood of waterlilies flat and green before us) on the twenty-first of January when he said, 'You know we are back in known land now.'

I glanced up at him from my hunk of Johnny cake. It was sour, and crumbled with the wet. But it was enough to make my belly stop aching for a while. He saw I didn't understand.

'I recognise the surveys,' he said quietly. 'Gregory and the other explorers have been here before us.'

'So,' said Burke, trying to smile. 'We are nearly there. Almost at the sea.'

Wills nodded.

I thought: *There is nothing more for us to discover then. We've found no lake. No lush grasslands for rich farms. We've found sand and rock and leeches . . .*

But of course I didn't say the words aloud.

We packed our tents then, onto the camels. We kept on going. We had set out to walk from coast to coast. And so we would.

On the ship, travelling to Australia, I had daydreamt of that moment. I had dreamt I'd see white-topped waves crashing on a beach. We'd toast each other, there upon the beach, a band of brothers who had done what no white man had before.

The reality wasn't like that at all. We never even saw the sea. Instead we came to a tidal channel and mangrove swamps, with mud that stank and tried to suck us down, while mosquitoes sucked our blood. No, I would never have daydreamt that.

The first white men to cross Australia from south to north. We had that at least, if we had nothing more.

But the journey north had taken two months — much longer than we'd planned. We still had to retrace the whole journey and find our way back to the camp at Cooper's Creek.

But our courage didn't fail us. We had got this far. We would make it back. Brahe would wait the four months Wills had asked him for. Two months to get here. Two to make it back. But we had brought only enough food for three months, at the most. But none of us had come for a doddle in the park. We could do it . . .

And then it began to rain. Mud sucked at our feet. The swamp tried to swallow us. Mosquitoes feasted on us more than ever. At times the air around us was almost black with them.

We forced our way through swamps that had been dry land before. Some days we made a mile or two. On others we were too weak to walk at all. At last we made it back to the mountains. But even there floods blocked our way. We would wake in the night to the sound of rushing water and know we had to move the camels to higher ground.

The poor beasts were skin and bone. Their feet looked gigantic above their skinny legs, their eyes shuttered by exhaustion.

Grey's face looked like a skeleton's. 'I'm ill,' he muttered, as Burke yelled at him to get a move on. Burke cast him a filthy look. 'Stop shamming it, we're all in the same case. We keep going or we die.'

But the rain was nothing compared with the hunger. The desperate longing every time we ate to just keep eating, to fill our bellies just once more even if we never ate again.

Grey killed a snake — eight feet long, it was as long as me and half again, weighing eleven and a half pounds. We baked it on the fire and stuffed ourselves that night. The meat tasted good. But all the next day found Burke shivering and sweating in his tent, his face green.

'That b—— snake,' he swore, then staggered from the tent. I heard him being sick against a tree. He was still ill the next day. But we had no days to spare. Our cheeks were sunk with hardship and starvation. The old leech bites still itched. Some swelled with infection and oozed pus.

Then back to Burke's River — that was where Mr Wills found Grey behind a tree, slurping up a gruel he'd made of flour and water. Wills checked our stores. Other things were gone as well. Mr Grey must have been helping himself the whole time we were plodding back.

Wills called Burke. He and I had both been trying to load up Rajah. The other camels were too weak to carry much. But Rajah seemed unstoppable.

'What is it?' demanded Burke.

Wills pointed to the billy of gruel in Grey's hands. 'I've checked the stores,' said Wills quietly. 'There's other stuff missing too.'

'I had to steal it,' whispered Grey. 'It's eat or die. I've had the runs since we left the Gulf.'

Burke clenched his hands. But he said nothing.

'I'm sorry,' said Grey desperately. 'I'm sorry, sorry ...'

Burke's fist smashed into his face. Grey screamed.

Smash, smash ... both fists now, pounding left and right.

Grey cowered to the ground, trying to protect his face. Burke seized him by the collar, and forced him up. His fist crashed into Grey's stomach. Grey began to retch.

'For Christ's sake, stop it, man!' I yelled. I tried to pull Burke away.

Burke lashed out. One fist caught me below the eye.

Grey lay moaning on the ground. Burke stood there panting, then lifted up his leg to kick him. Wills grabbed one of Burke's arms and I held onto the other.

'Let me go, Goddamn you!' Burke struggled like a madman between us.

We held him till he grew calmer. Grey groaned, and tried to rise. It took him two attempts. Bloody froth oozed from his mouth. Finally he limped over to the creek, and washed some of the blood away.

I looked at his face as we staggered on next day. The bruises shone green and purple. The shadows under his eyes were black. I believed he had the dysentery. But we did too. You do not steal food from your friends.

You do not strike your leader either, said a voice. Was it mine? At times the world swam and wandered in front of me. Fever dreams flashed through my nights, and left me damp with sweat.

How many days till Brahe would leave Cooper's Creek now, I wondered. Wills had stopped giving us the date each morning. We were already pushing ourselves as hard as any man could do.

The camel Boocha couldn't keep up. We stopped to slit his throat. We cut what meat we could, ate some of it half raw, just warmed up by the fire. We kept on going.

Grey stumbled. He tried to rise, but could get no further than his knees. Wills and I lifted him, and tied him across Rajah. He lay there limply, gasping.

Burke said nothing. We plodded on.

The sun ate the days. The cold froze our bones at night. Grey grew weaker. We had to lift him from the camel each night, and tie him on each morning.

Wills spooned flour and water into him. Grey gulped it like a baby. But he was mostly too dazed to speak.

Each day I wondered how long the camels could keep going. How long had it been since they had eaten? Gotch stumbled, unable to get up a bank. We killed him, then Golah Sing too.

We had no strength to carry most of the meat, and Rajah had Grey's weight to carry too, as well as our water. We dried what flesh we could in the sun. Hard black strips, but they'd keep us alive.

Perhaps.

Only Rajah and Landa survived now to carry Grey,

our food, our water, our blankets and our tents. But somehow Burke's horse Billy still stumbled on.

How could any horse take what he'd endured? His ribs almost poked through his skin. His hide was bare in patches. Infected bites oozed pus.

We were no better.

We'd made it halfway through the stony desert when Burke looked up. We had no fire tonight — no wood, no energy, no time for anything but walking and survival. Burke looked at Billy, his head dropping to the grassless ground.

'He won't make it back across the stones. I'll kill him tomorrow, while there's meat on him.'

Burke shot his horse in the predawn light. Wills and I helped him cut up the meat. Grey stayed in his tent, asleep or half unconscious, mumbling too low to understand. Billy's meat was sweet, but there wasn't an ounce of fat on the poor animal.

I glanced over at Burke. He had shown no emotion at Billy's death. He showed none now.

Grey had fouled himself. I helped Wills clean him. There was no spare water. But we did our best.

It was a few days afterwards that I found Mr Grey dead, cold in his swag when I tried to wake him. So he hadn't been shamming when he'd said he was ill. I wondered if Burke might cry for a man, even if he wouldn't for a horse. But he didn't. We scratched a shallow grave and buried him, and pressed on.

CHAPTER 42

The Camel's Story

Cooper's Creek, March 1861

At last the days began to grow cooler once again. Lightning cracked across the sky. Rain fell, though not enough to wet the dust. At least the air smelt sweet for a few seconds, covering up the smells of men and horses.

Every day one of the men climbed the hills and looked towards the north. Were they looking for Mr Burke? Every night I climbed the hills too. I stood under the bright stars and sniffed the air, hoping to catch a whiff of Rajah. But there was no smell of other camels in the air.

CHAPTER 43

John King's Story

Near Cooper's Creek, 21 April 1861

It wasn't far to the Cooper now. We would be there by the end of the day! We pushed ourselves through this last stretch, determination overcoming the weakness of our bodies, taking it in turns to ride the camels, forcing ourselves to get there before the dark, staggering as the afternoon shadows grew.

Landa and Rajah were nearly as weak as we were. Our only remaining stores were one and a half pounds of meat — all that was left of poor Billy.

It was Wills who first saw the line of trees that meant the river. We pushed ourselves harder than I had ever thought possible before. Step after step after step, even the camels plodding faster now, as they could scent the water. Our only thought was of that moment when we would reach the camp. Only a few horses to go . . .

CHAPTER 44

The Camel's Story

Cooper's Creek, 21 April 1861

Suddenly the men began to move. They packed up stores. They dug a large hole near a tree, big enough for almost half the sacks of food. They buried all the good oats and flour that could have been fed to camels. They carved shapes into the nearest tree, above the good food that they had buried.

Finally Dost Mahomet loaded us with all that remained, the tents and tools as well as bags of water.

No, young camel, I do not know why we waited there, with no grass and no good water. I do not know why we left that morning either. Men are strange!

CHAPTER 45

Dost Mohamet's Story

Cooper's Creek, 20 and 21 April 1861

We waited four months and five days before we left, four hungry men, and six starving camels, with skins slack from lack of food.

Each night Mr Brahe ordered a guard kept on the supplies in the stockade, in case the black-skinned people took them. The water stank. Green scum floated along the edges. Our flour grew sour and the rice grew mould. All of us grew ill, Mr Patton worst of all.

One by one we climbed the sandhills, and gazed towards the north. No one admitted they were looking for faint figures staggering back across the dust. We would stand till the heat drove us back to the waterhole and the thin shade of the trees.

Once I thought I saw them, men striding through the dusk towards our camp. I opened my mouth to give a cry. But then I looked again.

They were black-skinned men, not men with camels. They must have been hunting, for they carried something. But it was too far away to tell what it might be.

My stomach screamed at me in hunger.

Finally one night Mr Brahe made the decision. 'We leave tomorrow.'

No one argued. We had all known it had to come. Mr Burke and the others had either died, or decided to try to reach a town or homestead some other way. And if we did not leave now there would not be enough food to last us till we reached Menindie.

If we did not leave now Mr Patton would die, and then the rest of us.

I thought: *Mr Wright is dead. Belooch is dead. They have tried to get food to us across the shrivelled grasslands, and they have died.*

And without grass, without the camels to carry food and water, we were dead as well.

We left soon after dawn. Four thin men, one dying. Six camels, one almost staggering with the itch. We had left half our poor supply of food, buried beneath a tree. Half for us to get back to the Darling. Half for the four explorers to the north to get back too.

But they will not return, I thought. *The food would rot there under the hot ground.*

We had waited as long as we could. *No one,* I thought, *can ever say that we abandoned them.*

CHAPTER 46

John King's Story

Cooper's Creek, 21 April 1861

'I can see the tents!' yelled Mr Burke, running ahead of us.

But when we got there they were only shadows in the dusk.

They had abandoned us!

I leant against a tree, too weak to stagger to the waterhole and drink, though my tongue was swollen and my lips were raw. Flies sipped at the heat blisters on my hands.

Had it only been four months since we had left? It seemed I had lived a lifetime since I had seen this waterhole.

Had it always smelt as bad?

There was nothing here. Nothing but the silence aching all around us, nothing but our panting as we gazed around.

'Bastards. Bastards,' muttered Burke. 'Abandoning their leader . . .'

You said to leave, I thought. *You said 'Wait three months and go.' It's been four months now, and five days.*

But there was no point saying that to Burke.

Mr Wills saw it first — the blaze cut in the tree.

All that was left were words carved onto a coolibah tree:

Dig. (under)
3 ft *9ft* *40ft*
NW *NE SW* *W*
21 April 1861

So we dug — and found a camel feedbox filled with provisions: flour and oatmeal, rice and meat. With it was a note from Brahe, saying he had abandoned camp to go back to the Darling. Wright had not arrived. Patton was ill, the other three still well.

I looked at the date again, and tried to make my battered mind work.

21 April . . . today!

They had only left that morning!

If we hadn't stopped to bury Grey . . . if Burke had managed to walk that one day after eating the big snake . . .

But there was no point thinking of 'what ifs' now.

'They have betrayed us!' roared Burke. 'The traitors! Abandoning us here!'

I said nothing.

Brahe had waited even longer than we had asked. Waited till his supplies were almost gone and he was sure we were dead, I supposed.

Burke should never have left the stores and men behind. He should have sailed up to Menindie, so we started fresh. He should have waited till the cool of winter ... I shook my head, to clear it of the thoughts. The past was gone. What mattered now was our survival.

Burke was still muttering, half in rage and half in confusion from the sun and the diarrhoea that still affected us all. I managed to crawl to the waterhole, and bring us back a billy full of water to drink.

We felt better after that. The night air was cooler too.

Burke wanted to head after Brahe at once. But Wills was done for. I was not sure how far I could stagger either.

Perhaps tomorrow, I thought. *We will see what we can do tomorrow* ...

CHAPTER 47

The Camel's Story

South of Cooper's Creek, 22 April 1861

We began to walk back the way that we had come. There were six of us camels now, twelve horses and four humans, a small caravan after the big ones I had known.

It was not too bad at first, though Beer and Jambel were so weak they could hardly walk, much less carry packs with the humans' tents and food. But soon we reached the waterhole where we'd camped before. There was grass to eat there, too — the best grass we had eaten in a long, long while.

But we didn't stay, despite the water and the grass. My nose was telling me the plains that had fed and watered us so well on the way here were dry and dusty now. But these men had never learnt to listen to their camels. And if Dost Mahomet tried to give them good advice, they did not listen to him either.

The world grew drier. The creeks had shrivelled

into the ground. The grass had baked to dust. At times it felt as if we would become dust too.

Beer whimpered in the night.

We walked.

I do not know how long we plodded on. Each day seemed like the one before it. And then suddenly I smelt . . .

Camel!

No, not the ones in our poor caravan. But these were camels that I knew! I smelt Nero, Rangee, Shadow, Gobin . . .

'*Grahhh!*' I bawled. I stamped my feet. I was desperate to find these other camels. I could smell that they were near water, too.

But none of the men took any notice! The other camels harrumphed just like me. But there was nothing we could do.

Finally Dost Mahomet saw fresh camel droppings in the sand. 'Sahib! Look!' he yelled. And at last the men began to realise the truth of what I had tried so hard to tell them.

CHAPTER 48

Dost Mahomet's Story

Bulloo waterhole, 29 April to 14 May 1861

My mind wandered. I was following the caravan at home, the camel droppings on the ground. Soon we would pray together. There would be rice on the platter, a giant pile, with so much roast goat that the meat juice ran down onto the ground . . .

The camels snorted, and poor Bell Sing had to bawl and stamp at me before I realised . . .

Camel droppings in front of us, not behind. Camels . . . Belooch . . . Mr Wright . . .

I felt like crying like a baby. We had not been forgotten! They had survived! And so would we, for they were bringing food, the sheep that Mr Wright had said he'd buy. My stomach hungered for the taste of fresh killed meat . . .

It wasn't long before we saw their camp, shimmering in the hot air like a mirage on the horizon. There were trees about a waterhole, a rough stockade like the one that we had left behind, tents and camels and, as we drew closer, men who saw us and came running. I recognised Belooch, even at this distance, in his robes and turban.

Then I saw the graves. You cannot miss where men are buried. What other reason could there be in this desert to dig three holes like that?

'Dost Mahomet!' Belooch embraced me. There were tears in my friend's eyes. I stared at him. He was as thin as we were — worse perhaps. His eyes were like black holes. Empty skin sagged beneath his cheeks. Our rescuers were in a worse state than we were.

Around us the other men were greeting friends, exclaiming and explaining. I gestured at the graves.

'Who has died?'

Belooch took my hand. How long had it been since I had felt the touch of a friend's hand? 'Old Dr Becker. He died this morning. It is the will of Allah, my friend. Mr Stone and Mr Purcell are dead as well.'

My heart felt emptiness. I had not realised how much I liked the old man, with his bottles of strange lizards, his wrinkled hand guiding the charcoal to make his sketches. He had joined the expedition to find new insects and animals, to record what we had done in the pictures in his notebooks. He had stayed to work like all the other men, forced by Mr Burke to trudge in the heat and dry despite his age, only allowed to make his drawings at night after all the other work was done.

Now he was dead. There would be no more sketches. *Was this the hand of Allah*, I thought, *a punishment for making images of His creation?*

Then I remembered the lime juice, the stores left behind, the old man's words. 'If you die of scurvy in the desert you will know who to thank.'

It was Mr Burke who had done this.

No, this was not the rescue I had dreamt of.

We plodded over to their camp, and Belooch explained. It had taken months for money to come from Melbourne, for Mr Wright to buy fresh stores. Mr Wright had stayed to send his family down the river to Adelaide, as well. By the time Mr Wright and the others set out to find us the grass had withered; the waterholes turned to green mud. They had no surveyor with them, so they got lost. Their filth and poor food had made them ill . . .

They had eaten most of the stores that had been meant for us by the time they found this waterhole. Wright's men built the stockade to keep the black-skinned men away in case they attacked the weakened men or tried to kill the animals. Three men had died so far.

I glanced at the sun. It hung in the air like the gong Mr Burke had been so proud of, to call us to his side. It was time for us to pray again.

What would Allah send us now? How had I come to be here, led by men who knew so little about the land they could not find food or water, or even find the way?

Could we get back to Menindie?

We were in Allah's hands now, to live or die.

I went to cleanse myself and make my prayers.

Now we waited at the camp while Mr Wright and Mr Brahe went back to our camp on the Cooper, to see if Mr Burke and the others had returned there since we had left.

My legs began to swell, though the rest of me was thinner than a stick.

'Scurvy,' said Belooch softly. Dr Becker had told him the signs. Belooch's legs were swollen too. The water stank, and so did the air about the camp. I wrapped the end of my turban about my face, as much to keep off the bad air as the dust and heat and flies. All of us had diarrhoea now. Mr Wright and Mr Brahe came back, and said there had been no sign. Mr Burke had perished in the desert.

So we set off again, leaving the mud of our waterhole, the dusty graves, the stockade the men had built as though to keep off fever and starvation, as well as the men with darker skins. The horses staggered, and the camels limped.

We were skeletons that walked, thin men with dry lips and red-rimmed eyes, under a baking sky. Only the flies were interested in us now.

Some of us might live to reach Menindie. Perhaps.

CHAPTER 49

The Camel's Story

Bulloo, heading towards Menindee, May 1861

We began to walk again, into the dry world, back the way we'd come. There was no grass. Few bushes even for a mouthful of dry leaves. Even I was starving now. My knees trembled. My hump flapped against my side like a dry leaf.

I had never imagined a caravan could be like this. The horses sweated and shook with every step. The flies gathered at their eyes. The men walked as though the world about them were a dream. Even I was shaking with each step.

I looked at the dead limbs of the trees that had fallen on the ground. They were grey and white, like dappled bones. I wondered if Rajah was nothing but bones like this. I wondered if soon that was all I would be as well.

Dost Mahomet staggered as he tried to round us up each morning now. But we camels staggered too, so we were well matched.

One morning Dost Mahomet rubbed his mouth with his sleeve, as though his teeth hurt. Suddenly there was blood on his sleeve. Three teeth fell into the sand at his feet.

Dost Mahomet stood there, staring down at them, then felt up in his gums where they had been. His hands were swollen now, and his eyes looked tiny in his swollen face.

'What is it?'

It was Belooch. His skin was covered in big sores. The flies clustered round them even though he kept brushing them away.

Dost Mahomet gazed down at his teeth again, then at us starving camels, the high glare of the sky and the stony ground.

He smiled. It was a strange smile. I could see the black gaps where his teeth had been. He laid a swollen hand on Belooch's shoulder. 'We must trust in Allah,' he said quietly. 'For now there is no one else to trust.'

That was the day the first horse died. As you know, I do not admire horses. But even I could find no joy at the sight of that pitiful creature, its ribs protruding out of its coat as it lay panting on the hot bare ground, staring at its master with wide eyes, as though pleading for the water and the grass it had been so long without.

Beer died that night. She had been screaming with the pain from the itch. Then she no longer screamed. I was far away, hunting out the few last tussocks of dry grass, but as dawn became a grey light in the sky and Dost Mahomet slowly rounded us up, I saw her, lying on the sand, as still as a sandhill and almost the same colour, her belly already swollen with death.

The dreams of freedom came back to me. If I had had the strength I would have run right then, or stumbled, away from this horrible caravan and the crazy men that ruled it. I would have followed the faint smell of grass and water on the wind. Dost Mahomet and Belooch were the only ones who might have caught me, and these days they were so weak that they saw the world through a haze of pain.

But I was too feeble to escape when I was hobbled, or to break away when I was led. It took all my strength just to find a mouthful of tussock, and to plod on . . . and on . . .

Barra screamed with itch pain. Two more horses and four more men died too.

One human was too weak to walk much. Mochrani carried him. He was one of the camels Belooch had brought up from Menindie. He was the biggest camel now, apart from me. But he too was sagging skin. His big feet looked like clumps on sticks.

Dost Mahomet's skin sagged on his bones. My friend's eyes seemed too big for his head.

Friend? Yes, young camel, Dost Mahomet was my friend by now. You ask how I could have a man as a friend? Well, he did his best, even if he was no camel. What better can one say?

That morning his hands trembled as he reached down to untie my hobbles. Suddenly he gave a cry. He stopped, and put his hand to his mouth. He spat something out upon the ground.

It was another tooth.

It lay in a little froth of blood on the hot dust. He stared at it for a moment.

'We die here,' he whispered to me. 'Men, horses, camels . . . all of us will die.'

Dost Mahomet reached for my hobbles again. I stood still and allowed him to take my lead rope. I didn't kick at him. I didn't spit.

Where was my dignity, you ask? Where was my pride, my urge to show I was no man's servant?

You do not understand. But Dost Mahomet did. He took my lead rope and then he smiled at me. His teeth looked brown and bloody in his swollen face. His eyes were sunken into brown shadows. He stroked my neck for just a moment. Then he led me to the caravan again.

CHAPTER 50

The Camel's Story

Heading towards Menindie, May 1861

The days went by. There was no water and no grass, only scattered tussocks baking on the ground. We didn't walk. We staggered.

I was docile with Dost Mahomet now. I was as gentle as I knew how. I watched as he grew even thinner, his arms like the twigs on the drooping trees.

The dingoes howled. They would feast when we were dead. The land under our feet cracked with dryness, so it hurt our feet to tread on it. Even the ground was crying out for moisture now.

And still we plodded on, into dryness.

CHAPTER 51

Dost Mahomet's Story

Returning to Menindie, May 1861

We were dead men, who had been waiting for dead men, men swallowed by the desert, just as we would be.

I had only two comforts. The first was Belooch. At least we could pray together, he and I, though there was no water to cleanse ourselves as it is written. Instead, each prayer time we laid down our mats and built a cone of sand, the cleanest we could find. We prayed that it might be cleansed for our use, then we rubbed the sand across our skin as though it were water.

If only I could drink sand like water too, I thought. *If only I could eat it.*

At times it was impossible to pray five times a day, for the other men in the party would not stop. But every day we prayed at sunrise, at noon when the sun stood blazing up above and the shadows shrank to nothing on the ground, and then again at sunset, that blessed time when we knew we would have some hours of relief from that thief the sun, sipping at our moisture, drying out the world, our lives . . .

But on Fridays we prayed five times, as it is required. It was hard, out there, to keep track of days. At times the world swam as if we were under the water we craved. At those times it was hard even to remember where we were, to walk and keep walking, to bring the camels in and take them out . . .

Yes, it was hard. But we remembered, no matter what the sun might suck away, or the sand erode.

My second comfort was the camels. At times, as they plodded across the sand, I could almost imagine I was part of my father's caravan at home. Bell Sing would snicker, just as my father's favourite camel had done. The smell of dung and camel hide, the sweet sour breath as they chewed their cud . . . I could almost believe that my mother was waiting for us in the courtyard far ahead, her flatbread steaming as she pulled it from the dusty oven. Then I would realise it was only the hot sand that smelt of baking bread.

No, I thought, *if my father led this caravan he'd let the camels have their heads. They'd smell out water, if there was any in this wretched land. He'd let the camels go free, and we would follow them.*

That way we would live.

No man here would follow a camel. None would listen to a man like me, a man who wore a turban, whose skin was dark, who did not speak much of their language or know their ways.

Nero tried to gum me one night, as I put his hobble on. Once I would have rapped him on the chest, to remind him who was boss. But I had no heart for it now. The beast was half mad with mange, the bald patches on his skin red and shiny.

Bell Sing gave me no trouble now. Always before I'd had to keep an eye on him, in case he tested my authority again. But now we walked in friendship, he and I.

Friendship with a camel? But it was true. Every camel driver has a favourite camel. Bell Sing was mine. He looked at men as though to say 'You may lead me, but you do not own me. My soul is mine.' Bell Sing came from my homeland, like Belooch. Now he and I walked together. Perhaps we'd die together too.

CHAPTER 52

The Camel's Story

Returning to Menindie, 16 May 1861

It was still light when we stopped that day. No one had the strength to go further. My whole body screamed for water.

Perhaps, I thought, *there will be dew tonight*. If I could find some grass — any grass — there would be moisture. Not enough to soothe the craving. But enough to live another day.

Perhaps.

As soon as our packs were removed and our hobbles on I staggered out to find some food. Simla and the other females followed me. They knew I was the best at sniffing out a bush or two. The horses were too weak to come.

But there was nothing I could find. Not a tussock, not a thin dry bush. The world was nothing but rock and dirt.

I wandered further than the others that night. I hoped I could find food, could bellow to them to follow me, even though my nose told me I'd find nothing.

I was still out of sight of the camp when Dost Mahomet found me the next morning. He staggered across the cracked ground on his swollen legs, the lead rope in his hand. He undid my hobble chain, and signalled to me to sit. I did. He bent to fix my lead.

I was afraid for him. He smelt sick, a sour smell. Men should not smell like that.

A delicious breeze fluttered through the hot dry stillness. Dost Mahomet stopped.

He dropped onto the hot ground. He sat there next to me and looked out at the horizon. 'Do you know where there is water, Bell Sing?' he whispered. 'Can you smell grass on the far wind? Could you lead us there ...? It doesn't matter. None of these men will follow a camel. None of them will change the way they see the world, even if it means we'll all die.'

He gently stroked my neck. And then he said to me, 'Go with Allah, my friend.'

He walked away towards the dirty cluster of small tents. He didn't look back.

I stared at his dusty turban as it moved further and further away. What was he doing, leaving me alone? I took a step to follow him.

And then I realised.

My legs weren't in the hobbles. Nor was a rope tied to the peg in my nose. For the first time since I ran by my mother's side, nothing held me to the world of men at all!

I took a step. And then another.

I'm not sure what I thought at first. I was dull with thirst and hunger. I needed to find a tussock of dry grass and a tongue-moistening of dew. That was what my world was reduced to now.

And then I smelt it. Smelt the wind. Smelt a far-off hint of moisture, the scent of grass, just as Dost Mahomet had known I would.

I took one more free step, then another two. One step at a time I plodded towards the horizon.

CHAPTER 53

The Camel's Story

Central Australia, 16 May 1861

Night fell. The cool air cleared my brain. I walked faster now. No man would hunt for me at night. And by the morning I had to be far away.

Would Dost Mahomet look for me? Had he really meant me to be free?

I didn't know. I only knew that I must keep on going or they might find me. Might hobble my legs again or tie the rope back onto my peg.

I missed Dost Mahomet, though he had humbled me, like other men. *Even if I die*, I thought, *I am free of men.*

Step after step after step . . . My feet ached as they slapped against the hard cracked ground. I had to shut my nostrils as the wind blew grains of sand in my face, as sharp as tiny thorns.

I was so weak. Would I last another day, another night?

I saw a tussock in the distance, then some bushes too. Perhaps I should stop and eat, feel the moisture of the dew.

Stop and eat? Be captured, die?

Or walk without stopping, and die that way instead?

The desert breeze smelt of something else as well.

Freedom.

I kept walking.

CHAPTER 54

The Camel's Story

Central Australia, 17 May 1861

The sun rose the next morning, bright red against the redder dirt. The night wind dropped. The heat began to ripple across the ground.

But I knew where I was going now. I'd smelt water in the night.

The sun tore at my skin. It baked my flesh.

The world was wide on either side, red and bare.

But still I kept walking.

CHAPTER 55

Dost Mahomet's Story

Returning to Menindie, May 1861

We plodded on.

At times I heard the crows above us, screaming to each other, waiting for us to die. *The dingoes will eat us first*, I thought. The flies would feast, and finally crows would pick our bones.

One more man died. We buried him, though we were almost too weak to lift the shovels. Barra died. We cut off the shreds of meat left on her body, and dried them in the sun. There wasn't much. The bones were left where they lay.

I thought of Bell Sing. Was he still alive? Had he found grass out there, or water? Or had his bones turned white against the harsh red dirt as well?

I could hardly walk. Belooch helped me along. He was the one now who reminded me of the times to pray, who helped me kneel and rise. The sun was eating our flesh now. Would we dry to dust first, or would we die . . .

I shut my eyes. Belooch guided me as I stumbled. I dreamt even though I was awake. I saw Bell Sing, his big nose reach for leaves and munch them down.

I saw a well, my mother's face as she lowered the bucket, then drew it up again, filled with cool clean water.

'Dost Mahomet!'

It was Belooch's voice. I shook my head. I didn't want to stop my dream. Soon I would taste that water, sit with my father and my uncles on the carpet in the cool dark room. Soon . . .

'Dost Mahomet! Look!'

I opened my eyes.

At first I thought it was still my dream. A green fuzz on the horizon, like the mould on our stale bread. Trees. Trees meant the river, and Menindie. Beside us the camels' steps quickened as they smelt the water.

We had survived.

CHAPTER 56

The Camel's Story

Central Australia, 17 to 19 May 1861

I heard voices the second night, saw flames far off in the distance. It was the fires of the dark-skinned people. I left them alone, in case they speared me like a kangaroo. I hoped they wouldn't hunt me down.

I heard dingoes howl into the night. I saw a mob of 'roos bound across the sand dunes.

I did stop to eat that second night. Not much, but just enough. It kept me going the third day, and the third night too.

And by dawn on the fourth day I had found it.

It was a waterhole, a trickle between rocks into the sand. It smelt of birds and dingoes and every animal in this land that creeps or bounds. They had all drunk there this night. Now I drank too.

There was hardly any grass — the tussocks had been nibbled short by other teeth. But there were bushes and low branches that I could reach. I ate and kept on eating, and then I drank again. I stayed until I smelt rain upon the wind. I knew now which way I should walk to find it, and the fresh green grass that follows.

This was my land now.

CHAPTER 57

John King's Story

Cooper's Creek, August 1861

I never thought that black hands could be so kind . . .

I was too weak to eat today, but the old woman fed me gruel, scooping it up with a bark spoon and holding it to my lips as I sipped it. It was the nardoo gruel we tried to make ourselves. But we must have done something wrong, for what nourishes me now only made us weaker still.

It is hard to remember now what happened after we reached the deserted camp. It is like a dream gone sour. I can't even check my diary, as I buried it beside the tree, so the natives wouldn't find it. Strange to think now how afraid of them I was back then. Strange to think that savages can thrive here, while white men starve and die.

I felt better the day after Burke and Wills and I got back to the camp at Cooper's Creek. I wanted to press on after Brahe.

But Burke said no. The committee in Melbourne had told him there was a police station no more than one hundred and fifty miles away, at Mount Hopeless. It would take us a week at most to get there, said Burke. That was where we should go.

Wills agreed with me. He was our surveyor. Of the three of us he knew which way would be best. 'We need to follow Brahe,' he said. 'It won't be easy finding the way to Mount Hopeless through this maze of channels . . .'

But Burke glared at him, and Wills fell silent.

It was five days before we had the strength to leave the camp at Cooper's Creek. A group of natives arrived the day before we left. Burke yelled when he saw them appear like black ghosts through the trees. But when Burke went to relieve himself away from the camp they slipped through the trees and came towards us again.

I lifted my revolver to scare them off. But Wills ran to me, and pushed down my hand. 'They don't mean any harm,' he said. 'Look at their eyes, old chap.'

He smiled at the natives and gestured for them to come closer. They were carrying something. I gazed suspiciously. But it was just a big platter of cooked fish. Wills took it, just as we heard Burke returning. One of the natives gave a nervous laugh and they vanished into the black shadows of the trees.

Burke was still fastening up his trousers. He stared at the fish, and then at Wills and me. He must have known where the fish came from. But he said nothing. He ate his share as well.

The next day we began to walk, trudging along the creek bed. But Wills had been right. Cooper's Creek wasn't one creek but a hundred — a maze of channels, impossible to find our way through.

Landa soon got bogged in the wet sand. We spent two days trying to dig him out, using our hands and bits of wood. Rajah stared at us as we dug, and Landa struggled in the sand. For the first time I wondered if camels felt things like humans do. But we were too weak to shift a camel, and the poor beast too weak to struggle out. Finally we shot him where he lay, and dried what meat we could.

Rajah stood motionless in the thin shade of the trees while we dried the meat of his companion. Now and then he hauled down some leaves, or nosed at a tussock of grass. But there was little enough for even a camel to eat.

We set off again. Time after time we thought we had found the main channel, but it would take us out into dryness again. Time after time we were forced to retrace our steps and try again.

Rajah kept pace with us, even weighed down with all our food and water. It seemed nothing could stop the big beast, thin as he was, his skin rubbed bare in patches, sore and shiny.

It's silly, I know. But watching him plod across the sand, with our burdens on his back, I thought: *There goes one of the heroes of the Empire.*

Perhaps none of us was thinking straight by then.

Creek after creek, each one leading to the dry and earthy plains . . .

I had always thought of hell as flames. But this was another kind of hell, hot by day and freezing cold at night, and a maze of creeks that there was no escaping.

Rajah panted on, forcing himself forward with every step. At last even Burke had not the heart to drive him further.

We camped to let poor Rajah rest.

'Without help we're done for.' Wills spoke quietly as we sat around the fire.

Burke's chin rose with a little of his old spirit. 'Another few days and we'll be at Mount Hopeless. It can't be far now.'

Wills shook his head. 'By my calculations we're no nearer than we were when we started.'

Burke swore, still staring at the flames. He made no other answer.

At last Wills said, 'The natives will give us food. They're our only hope.'

I waited for Burke to object. But he didn't even look at us.

After a while Wills said in his quiet voice, 'I'll go and look for their camp tomorrow.'

Burke seemed to shake himself. 'Very well,' he said, almost with the old authority back in his voice. 'I'll come with you. King can stay here, and babysit the camel.'

'I can go alone ...' suggested Wills. But Burke glared at him and he was silent.

They left me at dawn the next morning. It was strange, sitting in the silence, a white man and a camel, each of us alone. I found myself staying by Rajah's side as he lay there on the ground, and listening to his panting. At time I even patted him. I hunted out leaves and grass and brought them back. But the big beast grew no stronger. Even his great heart, it seemed, had been destroyed by all that we'd been through.

It was hard when Burke and Wills returned.

'Shoot him,' ordered Burke, after a glance at Rajah.

It was the best way. Rajah was done for. But he had been a stalwart companion. For the first time in my life I had to shut my eyes as I pulled the trigger, unable to watch his placid gaze.

The natives had loaded Burke and Wills with all the nardoo cake, baked native rat and fish that they could carry in return for gifts of cloth. But when we looked for them again they had abandoned camp, leaving their gunyahs deserted. We slept in the gunyahs that night. It was a comfort, lying sheltered from the wind. The nights were cold now, and we were so thin the heat seemed sucked from our bones. The wind bit through our clothes. Even huddled next to the fire, one side of our bodies burnt while the other froze.

For days we hunted for the nardoo tree the natives used to make their cakes, but couldn't find it. Finally, despairing, with our rations a tiny Johnny cake and three sticks of dried meat a day, we came across a field of what I thought was clover. I looked closer and saw its seeds, and realised it was nardoo. At least now we knew we had food if we failed to make it to Mount Hopeless. We could camp by the nardoo and use it to survive till rescue came.

But we kept on going. Surely it couldn't be far now! If only it would rain! The heavens always shone that strange uncanny blue. Without Rajah there was no way we could carry water now. With no water there was no way to explore far, to find the way to Mount Hopeless. Never was a station better named . . .

After three days we returned to the creek, to the gunyahs, to water and the nardoo.

I collected more nardoo seeds and boiled them, as I had no way to pound them to make the flour the natives used. Later Burke and I found some rocks, and I pounded some of the seeds between two stones.

But it was hard work. My muscles ached. My head swam with heat and weakness. At times I thought I was back in Ireland, watching my mother pound the clothes on wash day. At others I was in the regiment, and the pounding was the beating of the drums.

At last we mixed the nardoo with our flour, just to get enough to make some cakes.

Each night we lay and watched the stars, and listened to the dingoes call.

'Perhaps they've come back for us,' said Burke, as we lay there in our swags one night, after our meagre dinner of nardoo. 'Brahe may have just gone to look for us. Or Wright — surely he will have arrived by now. We should head back to the base camp.'

I could hear the desperate hope in his voice. Hope flared in my heart too. Of course they would have come back, I assured myself. They'd be waiting for us now.

'I'll go,' said Wills. 'That way you can stay here with the stores. I'll be quicker by myself.'

I turned to stare at him in the faint light of stars and flame. *He means he'll get food from the natives*, I thought.

He was letting the side down, admitting our weakness to the natives. But Burke said nothing, so nor did I.

Wills left without saying anything the next morning. None of us had many words left by now. Partly it was weakness — words take energy, and we were well aware that we had none to spare. But mostly, I think, it was because the words we most wanted to say were unsayable — words of love and loss, words of anger over decisions Burke had made that had led us to our predicament.

I sat and watched the breeze ripple over the waterhole. It was deep here, the brown water dappled with dark shadows. Burke sat with his back to a tree, scribbling in his notebook. I closed my eyes and tried to think of home — the rich green of the hills around Dublin, the soft sound of Irish voices the sound of church bells on the wind. *Dear Lord,* I prayed, *let me live. But if I must die, let me die a true son of the Empire, true to my friends and to my duty.* And suddenly I thought I heard the whispers of the congregation as they prayed too.

I opened my eyes. There *were* voices! Suddenly I saw four native men, laughing as they strode down to the water. They carried spears.

Were they about to attack? I was about to yell for Burke — he was dozing too, by his tree — when I realised the natives were carefully ignoring me. Instead each cast his spear into the water.

They were such tall, strong-looking men. I felt thin and shabby beside them. Their arms were so very black as they pulled back the spears, each with a big fish wriggling on the end, and the sun was so white and bright above them. The whole land shimmered in the heat. The thought of fish made my mouth water.

I felt giddy with hunger. But an Englishman couldn't beg for food.

The natives noticed me staring at the fish. For the first time I understood the expression in their eyes. It was pity, and puzzlement too.

They laughed again, and offered me half their catch. I took it gratefully. Burke and I grilled the fish on the fire and ate and ate, cramming the food into our mouths, careful not to look at each other, each ashamed of our loss of self-control.

The next day the natives came again. They filled two big flour bags with fish for us. For the first time in months our bodies felt satisfied, and our minds were gentled by the plenitude of food.

The natives caught fish for us the day after too. But as they were leaving one of them poked his head into our gunyah. A piece of oilcloth that we'd used when loading the camels must have caught his eye, and he started to walk off with it.

'Hold it right there, you thieving savage!' It was Mr Burke. The native glanced up, startled, then began to run into the trees. Burke grabbed his pistol and ran after him.

The other natives laughed. They gestured for me to try fishing with their spears. I shook my head but they didn't understand.

Suddenly terror overcame me. I was a lone white man among the savages. Once more I remembered vultures hovering over bodies back in India, the natives who had smiled and smiled then murdered in the night . . .

I raised my revolver and shot it over their heads. Suddenly I heard Burke's pistol fire too.

The natives ran. I felt the breath seep back into my lungs.

Burke strode through the trees, grasping the oilcloth the native had stolen. 'Can't trust them an inch,' he said.

I nodded. My hands still shook. I hoped he hadn't noticed.

The shadows from the trees grew longer. I threw more wood on the fire. At least there was dead wood in plenty around us. I was afraid of what dark might bring. I cooked us a Johnny cake each on sticks over the flames, to eat with the nardoo. The Johnny cakes were good — they had that taste of real food, the food of home. But there was so little of it. I tried not to think of fish.

Suddenly I heard a noise behind our gunyah. I grabbed my revolver, and Burke snatched his, just as a voice called, 'White fellow! White fellow!'

There in the twilight was a whole mob of them, painted all over their bodies, carrying bark platters laden with cooked fish. They held them out to us, crying, 'White fellow! White fellow!'

For a moment all I could think was: *Where did they learn the English words?* Then terror overtook me.

'Up and at 'em!' shouted Burke. We ran at them, firing our revolvers. They dropped the fish and ran.

Burke grinned. It was the first time I'd seen him smile in months. 'Give 'em an inch and they'll be round the camp like flies the whole time.'

I nodded. *You must have respect*, I thought wearily. *You must be in control.*

Yes, I thought, *we've shown them.*

Shadows seemed to lurk around our tent that night. Mr Burke built the fire high. A spark flew onto the bark gunyah where we'd stored our food and stores. The bark flared up and the whole thing burnt to ashes. All our possessions gone within minutes, even our blankets! All we had left was our swags, a little flour, a revolver and a gun.

And our courage and our duty. I can say with pride that neither of us were lacking there.

We lived on the cooked fish the natives had dropped till Wills came back. I heard him first, tramping through the trees. It had to be a white man. You never hear natives approach, even when the bark should crackle underfoot.

'Have they come back for us?' I called. But I knew the answer even before Wills shook his head. If they had come back he wouldn't have been alone. He would have carried food for us. But his hands were empty.

'There's no sign that anyone has been there at all.' He had buried our journals there and left a note begging anyone who found it to bring us help.

He tried to smile. But deep down I think we all suspected no help could reach us in time now.

Wills had met the natives just after he left us. They'd fed him all the way there and back.

Exactly as I'd thought. But I couldn't find it in my heart to blame him. *Wills has never been a soldier*, I thought. *Wills doesn't understand how you must hold the fort, not let the side down, keep the natives' respect . . .*

'The natives' camp isn't far away,' he told us.

Burke stared at him. 'You're not suggesting we live with the darkies, man?'

'Why not?' Wills's open, friendly face looked puzzled. 'They obviously want to help us.'

Burke's face began to redden. He swore, and threw the natives' empty bark platter into the fire.

'It's that or die,' said Wills quietly. He stood up. 'I'll go and find them.'

'You will not!' screamed Burke.

I had never seen Wills defy his commander before. He did not argue now. He simply walked away, towards the natives' camp.

But the natives' camp was empty. Our revolvers had frightened them away.

We stayed where we were. We had no strength to move. We grew weaker, and weaker still. What was happening? At least we had enough food to fill our bellies. We ate pounds of the nardoo each day, as well as green, fleshy portulaca, a few crows I shot, and some small Johnny cakes as well.

Had the journey south so exhausted us that our bodies refused to accept food? We had had problems with our bowels for weeks. But it was more than that, I knew. A strange weakness had left us trembling and breathless, as though the land were stripping the last energy from our bones. Was this wretched country sucking the life out of our bones?

Wills's legs failed him. He could no longer even stagger to collect nardoo. Soon he could not even help us pound it. Burke grew too weak to collect the nardoo too. I had to gather enough spores for us all.

But I was weakening as well. My legs felt like sponge, all the water sucked away. My lips felt thick, so I had to force them to shape my words. My heart raced. It ached even when I sat and simply breathed. I couldn't even bend to harvest more nardoo.

'You have to find the natives.' Wills lay helpless by the fire but the flames hardly warmed the deep darkness's chill. The cold now was as capable a killer as the summer's heat had been. Dark bruises stained the flesh below his eyes. His voice was almost too low to hear.

I waited for Burke to yell, to argue and forbid it. But he said nothing. I struggled to my feet. I held out a hand to help him up.

'Leave me,' Wills began.

'Don't talk rot —'

'Leave me. Neither of you has the strength to carry me. The natives will help you back, to bring me food. There is no choice, old chap, no choice for any of us. You and Burke have to leave me here. You have to go.'

He was right. If we carried him we'd die.

'Are you sure, old man?'

He only smiled. I do not think I have ever seen a smile of such sweetness. 'Go,' he whispered. He handed me a piece of paper. The writing was faint and scrawled. 'For my father.'

I grasped his hand. It felt cold, even to my chilled fingers. 'I'll see he gets it,' I promised.

Wills smiled again. 'You always do your duty, King. Nobody can do more.'

I placed enough nardoo for eight days by his side, and flasks of water. Burke and I packed two days' worth of nardoo in our swags.

I made sure he was as comfortable as possible. The trees dappled their shade across his face.

'We'll hurry,' I told him.

And then we left him. When I looked back he was still smiling. He lifted his hand in farewell, then lay back and gazed up at the sky, as though listening to the birds at a picnic, back in the green fields of home.

I do not think I have ever seen such bravery. Even our trek to the Gulf did not demand such courage as this. To stay alone, too weak to move. To know that he might die alone.

That first day Burke managed to stagger through the drifts of sand along the creek. I helped him as best I could. But my legs still had that mysterious weakness too. The second day he said he felt stronger. But then he sank onto the sand. 'I'm done for.'

'No!' I pulled him to his feet. We staggered on.

One mile, two . . . Suddenly Burke threw away his swag. 'Can't carry it,' he muttered.

I said nothing. I threw away all I had too, even the nardoo, except for my gun, powder, matches and shot, so I could help him walk.

But he soon collapsed again.

It was impossible to stay here, on the sand, exposed to all the wind. The cold would kill us in the night. I forced him up. I carried him to the next small waterhole. I shot a crow. My body screamed with weakness but I forced it to pick and pound more nardoo. I made Burke a good meal, the best I could.

He ate well. But then he looked up at me and said, 'A few more hours, King, and I'm done.'

'No, sir!' I said. He shook his head. He handed me his watch and his notebook. He whispered, 'Stay with me. No man should die alone. Stay with me until I go.'

'I'll stay,' I said. I didn't try to argue with him. Death was in his eyes.

'Put the pistol in my hand,' whispered Burke. 'Don't bury me. Promise me that.' And then he muttered, 'You must save your strength.'

I nodded. I said, 'I will obey.'

He smiled at that. 'You always do.'

He was silent awhile, and then he said, 'We did it, didn't we? We walked across Australia. It wasn't a dream.'

'Yes, sir,' I said. 'We did it. They will still talk of us in a hundred years.'

He smiled again. He shut his eyes. I stayed until he died.

I left him unburied, just as he asked. Sometimes I dream I see him lying there, and the crows have pecked out his eyes.

I glanced at his notebook later. His last words read: 'King has behaved nobly . . . He has left me, at my own request, unburied, and with my pistol in my hand.' On another page he had written that we had fulfilled our task, but the depot party had abandoned their post.

The words swam. Sweat or tears? I couldn't tell. *Abandoned*, I thought. *They have all left me . . .*

No. One man was left. Wills . . .

CHAPTER 58

John King's Story

Cooper's Creek, August 1861

I kept walking. I slept in the natives' abandoned gunyahs. Loneliness weighed on me, like a stone I had to carry on my shoulders, but at the same time I felt light, as though the night wind might blow me away. One man by himself is nothing in the wilderness. You need company to feel that you are really there.

I shot another crow. The sound of the shot comforted me. It was the sound of civilisation, here in the emptiness.

I collected more nardoo. But all the time I was in terror that the natives would come, and steal my meat or my nardoo. I did not know what I feared more, to find them, or to stay alone.

I slowly found my way back down the creek to Wills. I shot three crows, thinking of his smile when he saw their meat.

But he was dead. Of course poor Wills was dead. I had known it all the time, had pretended to myself that he would be alive, waiting for me, that soon I'd hear his voice, another white man's voice.

His face was still turned up to the sky. He still smiled, too, as though he really had been far away, on that picnic back home.

The natives had covered him with branches. *He was their friend*, I thought. I took them off. I scratched out a grave for him. My fingers bled as I did it, the skin was stretched so thin.

I buried him in the sand. At least I buried him, like a white man, an Englishman, a member of the Empire. It was all that I could do for him.

I don't know how long I sat there.

The shadows clung to the trees when I remembered the letter Wills had pressed into my hand. It was almost too dark to make it out. Part of me felt guilty at sharing something so private. But it was so much comfort to hear Wills's voice as I read the words:

Cooper's Creek
27 June 1861

My Dear Father,

These are probably the last lines you will ever get from me. We are on the point of starvation not so much from absolute want of food, but from the want of nutriment in what we can get . . .

. . . We have had very good luck, and made a most successful trip to Carpentaria . . .

We had also every right to expect that we should have been immediately followed up from Menindie by another party with additional provisions and every necessary for forming a permanent Depot at Cooper's Creek. The party we left here had special instructions not to leave until our return — unless from absolute necessity. We left the creek with nominally three months' supply, but they were reckoned at little over the rate of half rations. We calculated on having to eat some of the camels ... We got back here in four months and four days, and found the party had left the Creek the same day, and we were not in a fit state to follow them.

I find I must close this, that it may be planted but I will write some more, although it has not so good a chance of reaching you as this. You have great claims on the committee for their neglect. I leave you in sole charge of what is coming to me. The whole of my money I desire to leave to my sisters; other matters I pass over for the present.

Adieu, my dear Father. Love to Tom.

W.J. Wills.

I think to live about four or five days. Spirits are excellent.

Spirits are excellent, I thought. *Yes, my friend. Through desert, flood and starvation, they always were.*

I was too weak to gather more nardoo. But then I saw the fresh footprints in the sand. *They will lead me to the natives,* I thought vaguely. I followed them, staggering from one to another. I shot crows and hawks as I plodded on, and tethered their feet to my belt.

The natives heard my shots. They took me and sat me by a tree. They brought me fish. They cooked my birds for me, and brought me the meat to eat. They took me to a gunyah to sleep with three other men.

I woke in the dawn to see black faces next to mine. But for the first time since the Mutiny I felt no terror. I closed my eyes and slept again.

That day they fed me once more. I made signs to show them I was alone, and that my friends were dead. They showed such pity. They were so very kind.

They tried to make me go downstream, I think to the outpost at Mount Hopeless. But finally I convinced them that I must stay with them. I moved camp with them. They made me a gunyah to shelter me. They brought me nardoo cakes and fed me meat from the birds I shot.

How can the natives wander so freely here, their children playing and laughing, when English heroes stagger through the heat?

I should feel like a hero who has walked across a continent, the hero I always felt destined to be. But instead I am a fretful baby, grateful for the hands that feed me gruel.

Tomorrow I will try to shoot a crow. It is all I can do to thank these people, all I can do to repay them.

This wretched, unforgiving country!

But I have never known such kindness.

CHAPTER 59

The Camel's Story

Central Australia, 1862

My new life was lonely at first. At times I even thought I'd welcome a (*phut!*) horse for company — yes, I was that desperate! I don't know how long I walked alone. The stars made their great shift across the heavens. The rains came and went, and still I walked.

But I grew stronger during those years. My hump swelled, my legs became tough with muscle. I grew to know the smells of this new country as well as my mother had known hers. The horizon held no mystery for me now.

At first I hoped that if I walked far enough I might find my mother's land. But no matter how far I plodded the scents were still wrong. Finally I accepted it. The Great Sea lay between those snow-topped mountains and me. The red sands and grey stone plains were my country now.

I was alone. But I was king. No dingo dared approach me. The kangaroos scattered when I galloped to a waterhole. Even the dark-skinned people pointed and chattered as I strode by.

But it's lonely, being a king.

Once I saw other camels in the distance. But they were in a caravan, all roped together, led by humans.

Was one of them Dost Mahomet, my old friend? I didn't know. But I did know I couldn't risk being chained up again.

I turned to stride the other way. Then something stopped me. The scent of other camels, perhaps. It had been so long since I'd smelt that.

I stopped. And then I planned.

I waited till the darkness was a blanket that covered all the world. Till the moon was just a trickle in the sky, like a seep of silvery water between the rocks.

I waited till the fires of the caravan were only glowing coals. I waited for the snores. I waited till the camels hobbled away from their camp, shuffling their legs inside the ropes.

And then I called.

For a moment no one answered. Then someone squealed back.

It was a female camel's cry. I could smell her now, that sweet stink on the wind. I called again.

Would she come to me? We would have to go slowly, with her hobbles. The men might catch us still. But it was worth the risk.

I heard footsteps in the darkness. Camel steps . . .

Unhobbled!

What had happened? Had they set her free?

And then she came closer, and I saw the answer.

This wasn't the adult camel that I'd smelt. This was a youngster, still smelling of her mother's milk.

She stared at me, her brown eyes wide, nervous and unsure.

The adult female called again. But it was not to me. It was to her daughter. Her mother was telling her to run. Now, while she was still too young to hobble, before the men realised she could survive without her mother's milk.

Her mother was telling her to run with me, and to be free.

And so we did. And she grew up. Other camels joined us, one by one — camels who broke free, camels who pushed against their hobbles, step by step, till finally their straps rotted. Camels like you, who ran before they thought to hobble you.

Camels like us, who follow the wind. Camels who are free.

CHAPTER 60

Dost Mahomet's Story

Menindie, 14 August 1861

I stood with Belooch on the veranda of the bakery, the smell of good fresh bread about us, and watched Mr Howitt's rescue party vanish into the world of dust and grasslands, the men, the horses and fresh camels.

Had it only been a year ago that we had strode out to face the wilderness like them? Now these men were searching for the lost explorers. Mr Brahe was with them.

'Could Mr Burke and the others really be alive?' asked Belooch, as we walked slowly down to the grass by the river where the camels grazed. My legs were still weak from scurvy.

I shook my head. 'Sandy and Frank may find their graves. Or men's or camels' bones bleached by the sun.' Sandy and Frank were black-skinned men. They knew this country, as the white men did not.

The camels snorted as we grew near. They were still weak — each morning I wondered if we'd find poor Mutwala dead. I brought down bread for them, a present from the good Ah Chee who owned the bakery. He was a Chinese man, an Unbeliever. But he had tended us when we were weak.

I smiled. Two years ago I could never have imagined having a Chinese as a friend. Who would have thought I would think a camel was my friend, either?

Sometimes I looked at the horizon, wondering if I would see Bell Sing plodding back across the desert. But all I saw was the hot air shimmering from the ground.

'I am staying,' said Belooch suddenly.

I stared at him. 'Of course. To care for the camels till Mr Howitt and his expedition come back.'

'No. In this land. For good.' He waved a hand, as though to take in the months of desert, the grasslands and the ranges. 'Bloom where you are planted, my friend. We are here. We should make the best of it.'

I shook my head. Not go home? To take my wages and be rich. To marry, to settle back in the familiar world, feuding with the clans across the hills . . .

There was nothing for us here. Nothing but adventure, and camels, and a country to explore . . .

I shook my head again. But this time I was laughing. 'I will think about it,' I said. 'Perhaps.'

CHAPTER 61

John King's Story

Yandruwandha Camp, Cooper's Creek, 15 September 1861

I was slumped against a tree in the shade when I heard the noise. At first I thought the sound of hoof beats was just another strange bird of this country. But then my native friends began to yell, waving and shouting at something in the distance.

I forced myself to my feet. I tottered over to them. There across the creek was a man on horseback. I blinked, but he was still there. Not a dream, not a mirage . . .

The man lifted his pistol. At once my friends began to run. They knew now what a pistol could do. I stood there, waiting for my rescue . . .

The man rode past.

He didn't recognise me! With my skin burnt dark, my tattered rags . . . he thought I was a native!

I fell to my knees. I lifted up my hands. I shut my eyes.

I prayed.

When I opened my eyes again the man was back. I tried to stagger to my feet. The man dismounted.

'Who in the name of wonder are you?'

'I am King, sir.'

He stared at me. 'King?'

How long had it been since I had spoken English? My lips found it hard to form the words. 'Yes. The last man of the Exploring Expedition.'

'What, Burke's?'

'Yes.'

'He looked at me as though he wondered if I were real. 'Where is he?' he demanded. 'Where's Wills?'

'Dead. Both dead. Long ago.' The world swayed about me. I fell onto the sand again.

Rescue ... I thought vaguely, as the man helped me to sit, went to fetch me food from his saddlebags. I would be a hero. The last hero, the one who had survived. They would cheer me down in Melbourne. My name would live for a hundred years.

But the dream shimmered, like the air above the hot baked ground. Instead I shut my eyes. I thanked my God, my comrades, dead in this harsh land. I thanked my friends, the black hands that were so kind.

I will tell the world, I thought, *of bravery and kindness. That story is my duty now.*

CHAPTER 62

The Camel's Story

Central Australia, 1873

I think of them sometimes, you know. The men from those far-off days. Did they all die in that desert — even my good friend, Dost Mahomet?

'Go with Allah,' he said to me. I hope that prayer was answered for him too.

I remember, I remember, but I do not understand. It's such a generous land you and I live in now. There are rains and there is grass, and even if you're human and can't smell it, you can learn to follow those who do.

I think of the dark-skinned people, watching those men in hats. The dark-skinned people stride across their world, almost like we camels do. I think of dingoes, kangaroos, of all of us, not just surviving, but flourishing in this good land.

Why couldn't those men listen? Why would they never understand?

But they were only men. Maybe, young camel, that is all the answer there is.

What Happened Next

The Camel

Bell Sing almost certainly did survive. Even though there were very few camels in Australia at the time, soon after the Burke and Wills expedition there were many accounts of stray camels seen in the distance and around station homesteads — a sign that those who had strayed from the expedition not only lived, but soon began to breed.

We know pretty much where Bell Sing came from. We know what happened to him and the other camels on the expedition. We know he wandered away on 16 May 1861. We don't know what happened when he vanished. But we can make a pretty good guess.

Bell Sing may simply have strayed. But the camels, like the men and horses, were extremely weak by then and were hobbled every night. I think that it's possible that Dost Mahomet did decide to give one of the camels from his homeland at least a chance of survival.

Bell Sing is probably one of the ancestors of the thousands of feral camels now contentedly wandering across central Australia.

Dost Mahomet

Dost Mahomet returned to Menindee (spelt 'Menindie' till 1918). On 3 January 1862, a big male camel called Nero, who had been on the first expedition, grabbed Dost Mahomet and lifted him into the air, perhaps dislocating his shoulder and breaking his arm. From then on his arm was either useless, or amputated — the records aren't clear.

Dost Mahomet went back to Melbourne. In July 1862 he put in a claim for compensation to the expedition, as well as claiming that Landells had promised him his fare back to Karachi and the same pay of £10 a month that the other men had been receiving. (The cameleers were paid either £6 a month, £3 a month or 8 shillings a month — the records vary.)

But he was never given the extra pay he'd been promised, or his fare home. The Victorian Government paid him £200 compensation, but that was all. The Expedition Committee, which had even paid for dandruff brushes and a candelabrum for the 'explorers' (i.e. the white men), gave him nothing. He was twenty-three, in a strange land and unfit for most work, including the job he was best at, working with camels. In his homeland men ate only with their right hands in the common food bowl and wiped themselves with their left. Life would not have been easy for a one-armed man.

Dost Mahomet settled back in Menindie and worked in the bakery of William Ah Chee, who also established one of the first market gardens in the town. Dost Mahomet died in 1880 or 1881, and is buried about a kilometre out of town on the road towards Broken Hill. His gravestone was erected in the 1950s by the local progress association, and the Central Darling Shire restored it in 2006. (If you are passing, leave some flowers there, for a brave man who died far from home.)

Belooch

Belooch remained in Menindie to look after Dost Mahomet and then went to Melbourne with him, where he too demanded his back salary and fare back to Karachi. Unlike Dost Mahomet, Belooch was paid first his salary, and then his fare back. He returned to Australia almost at once, though, in March 1863, bringing his wife with him. But she tried to return to India in August that year. She died on the voyage. He may also have been joined by Esau Khan — who may also have been his brother (or a different man with the same name as the Esau Khan of the expedition). The records are so few and so contradictory that it is difficult to be sure of the facts. Belooch was sometimes referred to as 'Belooch Khan'. But he was also called 'Ali Belooch' and 'Ali Black'. An 'Ali Belooch' probably would have come from a different homeland from a 'Belooch Khan', and had a different religion too.

Belooch seems to have been employed by other exploration parties. He is known to have travelled to Queensland to investigate reports that a camel had been seen near Mount Murchison and on the Barwon River.

Belooch and Esau Khan also joined Duncan McIntyre's Search Expedition to find the lost explorer

Ludwig Leichhardt. In 1886, McIntyre arrived in Camooweal and claimed he had found Leichhardt's remains.

I haven't been able to find out what happened to Belooch after that. By that time there were many more camels and cameleers in Australia. He may have started his own transport company, or joined someone else's. It would be good to think that one member of the expedition, at least, lived a long and peaceful life.

John King

After John King was rescued he returned to Melbourne a hero. He was given a gold watch and a life pension of £180 a year. But he died young, at thirty-three, exhausted by the hardships he'd endured both in Australia and in India.

George Landells

Landells's reputation was greatly damaged by the inquiry that was held into the deaths that occurred on the Burke and Wills expedition, even though he had resigned long before the end. After the inquiry he left Australia and went back to India, although I don't know if he continued to ship horses from Australia to India, or how he made his living. He died in Rawalpindi in 1871, aged forty-six.

Burke wrote few records of his journey; Wills mostly only wrote about the land he'd surveyed, and other records are scanty and contradictory. Even less was written about the 'sepoys', those men who were so essential to the expedition. I have had to choose which out of several versions of events were the most likely, or had to reconstruct what might have happened. And of course I have had to leave out many details we do know, or the book would have been too long.

Author's Note

Why did I choose a camel to tell the story of what's perhaps Australia's best known and most disastrous expedition? Partly because I wanted a happy ending — and there wasn't one for most of the men, or the horses. Partly, too, because camels have a certain look in their eye that says they have no very good opinion of humans ... and in the case of the Burke and Wills expedition, there was every reason for a camel to suspect that the leader didn't know what he was doing.

But mostly it was because I have watched feral camels in the outback, striding across a dry world with their eyes on the horizon, or — the last time I was there — standing contemplating the universe and their stomachs in a world of green and flowers.

Most of the animals that humans have domesticated, like dogs and cats and even milking cows and elephants, are happy to stay near their owners, either for love or at least the hope of dinner. But camels look as though they always dream of freedom, no matter what the burdens on their back — just like the camel in this book.

The Burke and Wills camels

By the late 1830s, as the British settlers learnt more about the arid inland of the Australian colonies, many suggested camels should be brought to Australia, as they might survive where horses couldn't and be able to pull or carry heavy loads where even bullock teams wouldn't make it. It was hoped that they would be able to take supplies to the scattered homesteads of the dry outback, especially in newly settled South Australia, and bring back wheat or wool, or precious metals from the remote mines.

Australia was already exporting horses and cattle to India, so it seemed logical to use those ships to bring back camels. The first camel to come to Australia arrived at Port Adelaide on 12 October 1840, from Tenerife. Its five companions had died on the voyage.

This may be the camel who became known as 'Horrocks's Beast' — the camel who shot his master. This camel's name was Harry. Harry was bad tempered, and bit people and other animals. He was bought by a pastoralist named Horrocks, who took him north on an expedition to explore the area near Lake Torrens in South Australia.

Horrocks was trying to shoot a beautiful bird on the shore of Lake Dutton when Harry lurched as Horrocks was reloading his gun. The camel's pack caught the gun's trigger. The blast shot off the middle fingers of Horrocks's right hand, then smashed through his cheek, teeth and jaw.

Horrocks was treated by a doctor but died of

gangrene just over three weeks later. Even though his injuries were due to his own carelessness, before he died Horrocks demanded that Harry be killed.

Other camels were brought to the colonies over the next twenty years, but the first large shipment of camels brought here was the one described in this book, which arrived in Melbourne in 1860.

The Burke and Wills camels came from what was then called the Northwest Frontier of India, an area that had seen many bloody skirmishes as the British tried to take control of a part of the world that many have tried to conquer without success — at least not for long. It is now spread over Afghanistan, Pakistan and the northwest corner of India, and still just as fiercely fought over.

The camels were bought in September 1859 by George James Landells, an ex-Indian Army man and horse trader who was employed by the Victorian Exploration Committee to buy camels and recruit experienced camel drivers.

Despite the Afghans' hatred of the British (and Australia was then a British colony), Landells travelled to Peshawar and what's now Afghanistan and managed to buy twenty-four or twenty-five camels and persuade eight cameleers to join him. He bought some of the camels at Lahore, which is still a major camel trading and racing centre, and is the second biggest city in modern Pakistan. But other camels may have been bought from smaller markets, or directly from the camel breeders.

Landells was supposed to buy both two-humped Mongolian/Turkestan Bactrian camels (*Camelus bactrianus*) as well as one-humped Arabian dromedaries (*Camelus dromedarius*). But he only bought the one-humped camels that we mostly have in Australia today. We don't know whether he just preferred dromedaries, or whether these were all he was able to buy.

The camel caravan walked about a thousand kilometres to the port of Karachi, where the expedition was joined by Private John King, a young Irishman who had some experience of camels in India. King had been ill and had been ordered to return to the cool climate of Ireland for his health — but he was to be the only survivor of the expedition into the harsh Australian inland.

The camels were loaded onto the SS *Chinsurah*. They landed at Port Melbourne on Wednesday, 13 June 1860, and were unloaded by the ropes and pulleys described in the book, in a weak and shaky state. They were taken to the stables at Parliament House, and then to stables at Royal Park. Another six camels were bought from entertainer George Coppin, who'd been displaying them in Melbourne, making the total cost of all the camel buying, transporting, feeding and housing about £5497 — an enormous sum for those days when a good wage was about £200 a year.

Some of the camels had babies while they were in Melbourne. Finally twenty-seven camels headed off with the expedition, leaving six behind — one big male, plus Landells's special pet camel, and two female camels and their babies.

Landells had complete control over the expedition's camels — but he didn't know all that much about them. He announced that camels needed rum and pepper to revive them when they were tired and had special shoes made for them for stony ground, which didn't fit. He was also paid £600 a year — £100 more than the expedition's leader, Burke. Most of the men on the expedition received £10 a month. The men who *did* know how to look after the camels — the Afghan cameleers — only received a fraction of that. They were probably the most skilled men on the expedition, but in those days very few 'white men' could accept that people with darker skin might know a lot more than they did.

The camels who set out from Melbourne included Bell Sing, Rajah, Golah Sing, Gotch, Landa, Boocha, Beer, Rowa, Mustana, Simla, Burra, Bunjib, Mutwala, Gobin, Coppin, Jambel, Mochrani, Nero, Janglee, Rangee, Shadow, Carlo plus five others with a confusion of names. (As I have said before, the records are both incomplete and contradictory.)

The camels weren't easy to get along with. They hated the horses — and the horses were afraid of the camels. The camels were constantly straying off to look for food, and a lot of time was spent hunting for them.

But despite this, the expedition would have been impossible without them. They carried the supplies when the wagons broke, and the horses were too thin and thirsty to work. But conditions were so bad — or at least so badly managed by the expedition's leader — that at times even camels couldn't survive.

One camel fell and dislocated its shoulder at Tarcoola on the Darling River when it was carrying two hundred kilograms, which is quite a weight on rough ground. It was left behind at Bilbarka. Another injured camel may have been left at Murray Downs Station, near Swan Hill.

Burke took sixteen camels north from the expedition's base at Menindie to Cooper's Creek. These were Bell Sing, Rajah, Golah Sing, Landa, Boocha, Gotch, Mustana, Beer, Rowa, Simla, Jambel, Bunjib and four others whose names we aren't sure of. One was left behind a couple of days before they reached Cooper's Creek.

There were now fifteen camels left. Three strayed or died while the men were exploring north from Cooper's Creek, looking for the best way for Burke to go north.

Burke took six camels on his dash north from Cooper's Creek — Rajah, Landa, Boocha, Golah Sing, Gotch and one other. They were all riding camels rather than pack camels, though Burke used them for carrying the baggage rather than for riding. They were all large strong males.

Four camels of these six perished on the way to the Gulf, either dying of exhaustion and thirst or being killed and eaten. Only two camels, Rajah and Landa, survived the journey up there. Both died on the way back. Rajah was the last one to die, on 7 May 1861, back at Cooper's Creek, as the three remaining explorers searched desperately for a way to the police outpost at Mount Hopeless.

Brahe was left at Cooper's Creek with six camels and twelve horses. One camel died of 'scab' — probably mange brought on by starvation — on the way back to Menindie, and Bell Sing, the hero of this book, went missing on 16 May 1861. When Brahe met with the reinforcements coming back up from

Menindie, they had either fifteen or sixteen camels with them (the records give different numbers).

Of the twenty-seven camels who left Melbourne, thirteen made it back to Menindie.

Some of those camels joined the fresh camels brought up from Melbourne and went with the relief expeditions that set out to find what happened to Burke and his party. Others would have been used as pack animals, and some may even have survived to help with the work on the Trans-Australian Telegraph Line — one of the nineteenth century's great engineering triumphs, which would have been impossible without teams of camels.

Loading a camel

A large, fit, strong camel can bear a load of up to five hundred kilograms, but such heavy weights are dangerous. Most carry about one hundred and fifty kilograms. (Burke tried to get his camels to carry about two hundred and seventy kilograms.) Camels are usually worked for about six to eight months at a time, then allowed to have a break to recover for the rest of the year.

Chewing the cud and gumming

Camels have thirty-four sharp teeth and can eat rough thorny bushes. They can give a savage bite, but can also 'gum' i.e. give a bite that doesn't break the skin. Camels usually gulp their food without chewing it. Later on they regurgitate the undigested food and 'chew their cud' — that is, chew it up before swallowing it again.

Feral camels

Between 1840 and 1920, thousands of camels were brought to Australia to open up the arid areas of central and western Australia. Some were riding camels; others were the big pack camels who could carry up to eight hundred kilograms on their backs. They included both the one-humped dromedaries and the two-humped Bactrian camels mostly bred for camel hair.

By 1920 there were about twenty thousand domesticated camels. But as the railways spread, and cars and trucks began to transport goods as well, the camels were no longer needed. Many had already escaped; now others were left to fend for themselves. They not only survived — they thrived and kept on breeding.

Feral camels can now be found throughout central Australia, in Queensland, Western Australia, South Australia and western New South Wales and Victoria. There are probably between half a million and a million of them. They wander looking for grass in the bushland and salt plain country in summer, hoping for thunderstorms, and in winter they congregate around the salt lakes and salt marshlands. They can easily travel seventy kilometres in a day.

Camels need lots of salt and like rough leaves and tussocks instead of lush green grass. They'll browse on thorny and salty bushes that most other animals won't eat, and can eat bushes up to three or four metres high. They can go for days or weeks without eating, too. A camel's hump is actually fat, storing reserves of energy, and in bad times they 'live on their hump', using the stored fat to survive (as the Burke and Wills camels did).

Camels do need to drink, though if their food is lush and green or the weather is cool they can go without water for days or even weeks. But if they're by a waterhole they'll drink at dawn and dusk, which is when most wild animals like to drink. They can drink two hundred litres in three minutes.

The amount of environmental damage done by camels varies. In good years they browse widely, choosing their favourite foods, and their broad leathery feet don't cause the sort of damage that the hooves of cattle, horses and donkeys do on fragile sand dunes and grasslands.

But in drought, when food is scarce, camels, like all other animals, eat whatever they can get. They can totally strip an area of all its young trees and bushes. And they are using food and water that could support native Australian animals. Many native Australian animals are rare or endangered and any competition for food or water may mean their extinction.

Wild camels are now captured for meat. It's low in fat and tastes a bit like beef. Others are caught and sold overseas as racing camels.

The 'cameleers'

Australia's first cameleers — and possibly the first 'Afghans' ever to come to Australia — were the eight cameleers Landells hired from the Indian subcontinent for the expedition.

Very little is known about what those eight men were like. We are not even sure of their names — many versions were given — or where they came from exactly, or even their religion — though some of that can be deduced from their names. But I think we can make a pretty good guess. They must have been strong and independent, or they would never have had the courage to come out here (especially after the bloodshed and bitterness of the wars with Britain), or stay once they'd got here. And they must have had a sense of adventure too.

At first the Australian cameleers were called 'camellias' or 'sepoys', which was what the English called Indians who worked for the British Army in India. Later the men who came out to work with the camels were usually known as 'Afghans'.

This term was used for people from a wide range of different ethnic groups, and from vastly different areas, like Baluchistan, Kashmir, Sind, Rajastan, Punjab and even Turkey, Egypt and Persia. Their families were tribal people, peasant farmers or merchants or nomads. Most were Muslims, though some camel handlers were Hindu, Parsi or Christian. And they knew all about working with camels.

Four of the eight cameleers hired by Landell decided to go back home once they got to Melbourne. Perhaps they were homesick, or perhaps they had begun to realise the lack of respect that men of their race would have to put up with at that time in Australia. Their fares to Calcutta were paid for by the committee that was funding the expedition. This left four to join the expedition — Dost Mahomet, Belooch, Esau Khan, who became ill and whom Burke fired at Swan Hill, and Simla, the Hindu who nearly starved because, for religious reasons, he couldn't eat the beef that was the expedition's main food. After three days of living on what Ludwig Becker, the expedition's official expedition artist as well as a naturalist and a prominent member of the Royal Society, said was only 'bread and plenty of work', Simla realised there was no way he could stay with the expedition. He was given his wages, but there is no evidence that he was given his fare back home.

Esau Khan returned to Melbourne where he was employed to look after the camels that had been left behind.

In 1865 an 'Esau Khan' joined Belooch Khan for Duncan McIntyre's Leichhardt Search Expedition. This may have been the same Esau Khan. But by then there were more cameleers in Australia, and it may have been a different man with the same name — especially as the Esau Khan of Burke's expedition was also referred to as Issah or Hissan.

Turbans

Turbans — lengths of soft cloth up to three metres long — have been worn by many cultures, and for many reasons — for some religious (those of the Sikh religion are required to wear turbans over their long, uncut hair), for others ceremonial or just practical.

The turbans worn by the cameleers weren't just something to wear on their heads. Possibly first developed as a thick head covering to protect the wearer during battle, the cloth could be wrapped in one of many patterns to show which tribe or village you came from, or sometimes what position you held in society. Flaps of cloth from the turban could protect the face and neck from the sun or wind, or flies or biting insects. In sandstorms the thin cloth could be worn over the face to keep the sand out of the nose and eyes, and the cloth was so thin that you could see through it, like a pair of goggles. At night the turban could be unwrapped to become a ground sheet or a light blanket. It could even be used to filter dirty water.

Most importantly for the three Muslim cameleers, a turban is worn high up on the head and allowed the wearer to touch their forehead to the ground when praying, in accordance with Islamic law. (Of course, not everyone who follows Islam wears a turban, either now or when this story is set.)

In some places turbans are made like hats, sewn together so they can just be placed on the head. But the cameleers would have wrapped their turbans on every day.

Artists' pictures of the Burke and Wills expedition show the cameleers wearing white turbans. In Afghanistan over a century later the Taliban would force men to wear black turbans.

The Yandruwandha People

The Yandruwandha occupied the area north of Cooper's Creek to Gidgealpa and south to Bollard's Lagoon. Their area followed Cooper's and Strzelecki creeks in what is now the northeast corner of South Australia and a neighbouring strip of Queensland. They had close connections with several other language groups, particularly the Dieri to the west and the Yawarawarka to the north.

The explorers' fear and mistrust of the Yandruwandha were entirely irrational, as the Yandruwandha never showed them any hostility. The Yandruwandha people did take items from the camp (and tried to take some oilcloth from Burke and King later) — possibly as part of what they would have seen as a form of exchange for the fish and other things they offered the explorers. But the explorers continued to refuse their offerings, even when they were starving.

Although introduced diseases and relocation during the 1900s means that there are no initiated members of the Yandruwandha alive today, their descendants still look after significant sites, and the Yandruwandha language is still used and taught. The Muda Aboriginal Corporation at Bourke has a Language Centre, and Yandruwandha is taught at preschool, primary and high school levels, as well as at the local TAFE.

In April 2007 the South Australian Minister for Aboriginal Affairs and Reconciliation used his powers to stop the sale of a breastplate found near Innamincka. The South Australian Museum believes the plate was one of three presented to the Yandruwandha people of Cooper's Creek by the Royal Society of Victoria in recognition of the compassion and generosity shown by the Yandruwandha people to Burke, Wills and King.

The South Australian Government also took the unusual step of setting aside land at Cooper's Creek, nominally for the exclusive use of the Yandruwandha people, but it was soon handed to a Lutheran community, who made a short-lived attempt to establish a mission station there.

The Innamincka Regional Reserve and the Coongie Lakes National Park have been created to help conserve both the natural environment and the middens (rubbish piles), tool manufacturing sites, rock engravings, burial sites, quarries and timber, stone and earth arrangements of the original inhabitants.

Why the Burke and Wills Expedition failed

Robert O'Hara Burke died of ignorance, surrounded by people who could have helped him survive. But Burke was a white man. He distrusted the local Indigenous people and the cameleers, who understood not just camels, but how a camel can find food and water too. He was also stubborn — and perhaps saw himself too romantically a 'hero of the wilderness' — to have let his expedition sail up to Menindie from Adelaide or even Echuca — a week's easy journey instead of the months of desperate slogging through the drylands. Burke's obstinacy and prejudice led to the deaths of himself and many other men, as well as his horses, dogs and half of his camels.

The Burke and Wills expedition should have been one of the greatest explorations ever. Instead it turned into one of the most pointless. (Perhaps if it had been the Wills and Burke expedition — if Wills had been the leader — it would have been different too.)

The Victorian Exploration Committee wanted someone to cross Australia, and uncover the mysteries of the inland — just like the Englishman Dr David Livingstone had been doing in Africa. What would they find? Were there vast lakes up there, or rivers and good grasslands? Could they make vast fortunes, taking their flocks up to the new land?

But the expedition was about more than money.

This was a time when the whole idea of exploring was romantic — the idea of white men pitting themselves against an unknown country.

In actual fact, the white 'explorers' usually had local guides to show them where to go. Even Burke's assistant, Wright, was helped by Indigenous guides like Watpipa and the man remembered only as 'Dick', who went with Trooper Lyons and Alexander MacPherson when they set out from Menindie to take official letters to Burke. Lyons and MacPherson became lost, but Dick took them to the local Indigenous people, who looked after them, while Dick walked for eight days (his horse was too exhausted to continue) back to camp to get help for them.

Burke and his companions died mostly because Burke was unable to get on with the local people who had been living there for tens of thousands of years. But in those days only what white male Europeans did really counted.

This expedition would be *big* — the first journey by Europeans right across the centre of Australia — if the explorers made it across and could return alive.

A Melbourne businessman contributed £1000 on the condition that the public gave £2000 too. And they did! And the Victorian Government put in £6000. This was an extraordinary amount of money in the days, about what thirty men would earn in a year. But this was soon after the Victorian Gold Rush. Marvellous Melbourne (also known as Smelbourne because the Yarra River stank) was full of money and self-importance.

The supplies were lavish too. The explorers set out with an incredible twenty tons of baggage. In fact, the expedition became a byword for luxurious and silly items. An axe could have done a far better job of marking the trees than the special branding iron with the words 'B/VE' — especially as the camels and wagons had to carry six tons of firewood too!

At first it looked like Colonel Warburton, South Australia's Police Commissioner and an experienced bushman, was going to lead the expedition. But at the last minute Robert O'Hara Burke was given the job instead.

Why? Burke was a Victorian police superintendent. He had never handled camels. He wasn't an experienced bushman either. But as an ex-military man Burke was supposed to be used to commanding men — and he was a Victorian, not a South Australian! He also had good political connections. There is a theory, too, that Burke promised the expedition's backers first go at claiming any rich farmland he discovered.

Burke was an appalling choice. He was impulsive, had a violent temper, and threatened the local people who might have helped the expedition — both Aboriginal and European. His record-keeping was so bad that we simply don't know why many of his decisions were made. If it were possible to make a mess of things, Burke did.

But most of all Burke was just a poor bushman, without the experience or intuition to look at the land around him and work out the best way to survive.

The second-in-command of the expedition was to be George Landells. He too had a quick temper, and was very protective of his authority over the camels, though in fact he knew very little about them.

Brahe dug up the boxes and saw that Burke and the others had been back. But because Burke hadn't thought to put another blaze on the tree to say to dig under the boxes, Brahe missed Burke's note saying which way they'd gone.

Brahe left no more messages at the 'Dig' tree. So a couple of weeks later when Burke sent Wills back to see if anyone had come looking for them nothing seemed to have changed. Wills buried his records and a note begging anyone who read them to send help.

What really did kill Burke and Wills?

Most of the deaths in the expedition were from starvation, or poor food, leading to scurvy or dysentry.

But Burke and Wills had enough food to survive. They actually died of nardoo poisoning.

Nardoo (*Marsilea drummondii*) is a water fern. It looks a bit like a giant four-leaf clover, with green leaves and red in the centre. Like all ferns, nardoo doesn't have flowers or seeds. Instead it produces spores. As the fern matures, its rhizome, or underground root, produces 'sporocarps', hard, starchy, nut-like clusters of spores about nine millimetres long.

The Cooper's Creek channel country is dry most of the time. But when rains fill the channels the nardoo plants spring up in great green carpets, and as the floods die down the plants leave their spores in the mud. When it rains again they too will spring to life.

When Burke, Wills and King began to prepare their own nardoo they ground up the plant — sporocarps and all — and mixed it with water into a thin paste, as they thought the local Yandruwandha people did.

But they'd missed a vital step. The Yandruwandha people roasted the spore cases before they ground them up on big flat grinding stones.

Burke, Wills and King ate about two kilograms of nardoo each day — it was just about all they were eating, apart from a bit of crow meat. But they grew thinner and thinner. Their legs started shaking too.

These days we know that nardoo contains an enzyme called thiaminase, which breaks down thiamine (vitamin B1). Without thiamine our nerves and brains don't function properly, and our bodies can't make ATP, a complex molecule that provides energy so our cells can work. Thiamine deficiency leads to the disease beri beri. Your hands and legs start shaking, you feel weak, your heart becomes enlarged and you slowly starve to death, even with enough food. When the Yandruwandha people roasted their nardoo they changed it from a toxic plant into an excellent and quite tasty food, used either as a thin soup or gruel, or made into cakes and baked on hot stones.

If Burke, Wills or King had watched the Yandruwandha people more closely they would have had enough food to survive till the rescue party arrived. They could even have asked the Yandruwandha for help to reach Mount Hopeless. But if Burke had been the sort of man who took advice, the expedition would have been an easy one, instead of a tragedy.

Burke's Achievements

The expedition which had started out with such grand hopes achieved very little. Even cattle couldn't long survive the repeated dry times in the new areas Wills surveyed. Not even a road marks the way they went.

Ironically the scientific data recorded by Dr Becker, Dr Beckler and gallant Mr Wills — who kept on recording and surveying even when he was starving on the way back from the Gulf — are probably the most valuable results of the tragic waste of life and effort, even though Burke disliked and insulted Dr Becker and Dr Beckler, and was contemptuous of their scientific efforts.

Burke's greatest contribution has probably been to Australian legends and stories. For many years he and his party were seen as tragic heroes, defeated by a harsh land. Later they were seen as lost Europeans, and Burke as a driven, disorganised madman. Probably neither of these is accurate — just as in this book all three of the main characters see Burke in very different ways. But Burke left few written records. He is now remembered mostly by the opinions of others.

Grey's Creek
Now called the Diamantina.

The Itch
Possibly mange, caused by small biting creatures, or hair loss due to starvation and overwork and infected scratches.

Johnny cakes
Basic ones were just flour and water baked on a stick over the fire, or fried in fat in a pan. Others had fat of some sort (butter, mutton fat) and sugar, honey or treacle added, or even currants. But King's were probably just flour and water.

Flour and water gruel (also called skilligee)
This was made for sick people, and supposed to be good for you. It's pretty horrible — just flour (or ground rice or potato flour) cooked with water. But Grey couldn't have cooked his without the others noticing, so he probably just ate raw flour mixed with water, hoping it would help stop his diarrhoea.

Fever
Take your pick! In India King may have suffered from malaria, typhoid, dysentery, cholera or several other illnesses that give you a high fever. The sick men on the expedition may have had what used to be known as Barcoo Rot, a (mostly) skin disease, or Barcoo Fever, also called 'Barcoo Vomit' or 'Barcoo Spews'. People with Barcoo Rot had sores over their body, sometimes fungal infections on their skins, swelling and weakness. It was caused by a poor diet and bad hygiene. People with Barcoo Fever had a high temperature, vomiting and diarrhoea. It may have been caused by blue-green algae in the rivers (the toxin is still there even if you boil the water). But they were also drinking water that was polluted by animal and human faeces, living closely with animals and not washing, so they may have had any one of dozens of bacterial, viral, fungal or parasitic infections. Poor food and bad hygiene were the killers, rather than simple starvation.

Cooper's Creek
Cooper's Creek is usually just a series of waterholes, some shallow, one twenty-seven metres deep, but when it floods deep water rushes into a maze of

channels. When the floods dry up only the channels in the sand are left, with no clear clue which is the main river.

The explorer Captain Charles Sturt named Cooper's Creek on 13 October 1845 after the South Australian judge Charles Cooper. There wasn't much water in it when he crossed it, so he called it a 'creek' instead of a river.

The Yandruwandha's use of English words

Even if none of the Yandruwandha had met English speakers before, they may still have known a few English words. The local Aboriginal nations had trade routes over thousands of kilometres, following what are now known as Cooper's Creek and the Diamantina and Georgina rivers. Sea shells came from the north, axe heads, ochre and spears from the south — and probably news of the new settlers too, along with a few words of their English language.

Memorials

Tourists can now visit the 'dig' tree, where Brahe buried the supplies — though it may be the wrong tree. There's a memorial cairn, twenty kilometres west of Innamincka, which is roughly in the area where William Wills' body was found by the rescue party in September 1861. There's also a memorial plaque where Burke's body was found, about eight kilometres east of Innaminka. (The rescue party took both bodies back to be buried again in Melbourne.) There is also a stone cairn with the words 'KING' in the area where King was found with the Yandruwandha people.

Acknowledgments and Thanks

The most fascinating pieces of stories of the Burke and Wills expediton are the bits we don't know. The records tell us how much they paid for firewood, but litle about nearly all the men on that doomed journey, especially the cameleers. I was lucky enough to have the help of Barry Hooker, author of *Indonesian Islam: Social Change through Contemporary Fatawa* (2003), *Islamic Law in South-East Asia* (1984) and *Indonesian Syari'ah: Defining a National School of Islamic Law* (2008). It is impossible to thank Barry enough for the extraordinary breadth of expertise he lent me so that I could work out the backgrounds of this extraordinary band of 'Afghans'. All errors are mine, not his.

And as always, so many, many thanks to the team who also created this book: To Lisa Berryman and Liz Kemp, who demanded I rewrite a story with humans, not just camels; to Kate O'Donnell, who has carefully guided each incarnation on its way; to Natalie Winter, for the magic of her covers; to Angela Marshall who turns a scribble into text; and to Emma Kelso, who as always slashed, mashed and suggested, and made this book far richer than it could ever have been without her.

PS: Many details in this story may conflict with material on the web about the expeditions, or even in one of the journals written at the time. Please don't write to tell me! Many of the documents written by members of the expedition (or those close to them like Wills's father, who wrote a book defending his son) contradict each other. As with most stories from the past, there are many possible versions of what happened.

Jackie French is a full-time writer and wombat negotiator. Jackie writes fiction and non-fiction for all ages, and has columns in the print media. Jackie is regarded as one of Australia's most popular children's authors. She writes across all genres — from picture books, humour and history to science fiction.

Visit Jackie's websites

www.jackiefrench.com

or

www.harpercollins.com.au/jackiefrench

to subscribe to her monthly newsletter

Some of Jackie's Awards

Hitler's Daughter

- CBC Younger Readers' Award winner, 2000
- UK National Literacy Association WOW! Award winner, 2001
- Shortlisted in the Fiction for Older Readers category, YABBA awards 2007
- US Library Association Notable Book
- Koala Awards 2007, Roll of Honour
- Semi-Grand Prix award, Japan
- The Helpmann Award for a Children's Presentation and two Drover's Awards, 2007, for the Monkey Baa production of *Hitler's Daughter: the play*

In Your Blood

- ACT Book of the Year, 2002

Diary of a Wombat (illustrated by Bruce Whatley)

- Nielsen BookData/Australian Booksellers Association Book of the Year, 2002 (the only picture book ever to win this award)
- (USA) Benjamin Franklin Award
- (USA) Lemmee Award
- (USA) Favourite Picture Book of the Year, Cuffie Awards, 2003
- (USA) Funniest Book in the Cuffie Awards (tied with *Diary of a Worm*), 2003
- Cool Award, for Best Picture Book, voted by the kids of the ACT, 2003
- Young Australian Readers' Award winner, 2003
- KOALA Award for Best Picture Book winner, 2003
- (USA) KIND Award winner, 2004
- Shortlisted for the Bilby Awards, 2007
- Northern Territory KROC Award for Favourite Book of 2007

To the Moon and Back (co-written with Bryan Sullivan, Jackie's husband)

- CBC Eve Pownall Award for Information Books winner, 2005

They Came on Viking Ships

- Shortlisted: (UK) Essex Book Award; winner to be announced in 2008
- Winner: West Australian Young Readers' Book Awards (WAYBRA) (Younger Readers), 2007
- Shortlisted: NSW Premier's History Awards (Young People's History Prize), 2006

Macbeth and Son

- Shortlisted: CBC Awards, 2007

The Goat Who Sailed the World

- Notable Book: CBC Awards (Younger Readers), 2007

Josephine Wants To Dance (illustrated by Bruce Whatley)

- Australian Booksellers' Book of the Year, Younger Readers, 2007.
- Notable Book: CBC Awards (Early Childhood), 2007
- Notable Book: CBC Awards (Picture Book of the Year), 2007

Pharaoh

- Shortlisted: CBC Awards (Older Readers), 2008

Shaggy Gully Times (illustrated by Bruce Whatley)

- Shortlisted: CBC Awards (Younger Readers), 2008

Other Titles by Jackie French

Wacky Families Series

1. My Dog the Dinosaur • 2. My Mum the Pirate • 3. My Dad the Dragon
4. My Uncle Gus the Garden Gnome • 5. My Uncle Wal the Werewolf
6. My Gran the Gorilla • 7. My Auntie Chook the Vampire Chicken
8. My Pa the Polar Bear

Phredde Series

1. A Phaery Named Phredde • 2. Phredde and a Frog Named Bruce
3. Phredde and the Zombie Librarian • 4. Phredde and the Temple of Gloom
5. Phredde and the Leopard-Skin Librarian • 6. Phredde and the Purple Pyramid
7. Phredde and the Vampire Footy Team • 8. Phredde and the Ghostly Underpants

Outlands Trilogy

In the Blood • Blood Moon • Flesh and Blood

Historical

Somewhere Around the Corner • Dancing with Ben Hall • Soldier on the Hill
Daughter of the Regiment • Hitler's Daughter • Lady Dance • The White Ship
How the Finnegans Saved the Ship • Valley of Gold • Tom Appleby, Convict Boy
They Came on Viking Ships • Macbeth and Son • Pharaoh
The Goat who Sailed the World • The Dog who Loved a Queen
A Rose for the Anzac Boys

Fiction

Rain Stones • Walking the Boundaries • The Secret Beach • Summerland
Beyond the Boundaries • A Wombat Named Bosco • The Book of Unicorns
The Warrior – The Story of a Wombat • Tajore Arkle • Missing You, Love Sara
Dark Wind Blowing • Ride the Wild Wind: The Golden Pony and Other Stories

Non-fiction

Seasons of Content • How the Aliens from Alpha Centauri Invaded
My Maths Class and Turned Me into a Writer
How to Guzzle Your Garden • The Book of Challenges
Stamp, Stomp, Whomp • The Fascinating History of Your Lunch
Big Burps, Bare Bums and Other Bad-Mannered Blunders
To the Moon and Back • Rocket Your Child into Reading
The Secret World of Wombats
How High Can a Kangaroo Hop?

Picture Books

Diary of a Wombat • Pete the Sheep • Josephine Wants to Dance
The Shaggy Gully Times • Emily and the Big Bad Bunyip

The Goat who Sailed the World

The HM Bark *Endeavour* is sailing to Tahiti to map the transit of Venus, but there are rumours that once the task is completed, Lieutenant James Cook has a set of secret orders — orders that command him to search for the Great South Land.

Isaac is twelve and has joined the crew of the *Endeavour* as a master's servant, good for scrubbing decks and not much else. He's certainly not considered good enough to fetch hay for the Goat who will provide fresh milk for Cook and his officers. And this goat even has more experience at sea than Isaac — she has already sailed around the world once, watching the ocean and lands slip by from her spot on the quarterdeck.

Over the months on board the *Endeavour*, a friendship grows between the Goat and Isaac, one that will last through shipwreck, bushfire and illness. A friendship that helps in the discovery of exotic new lands ...

The Dog who Loved a Queen

To the world outside her luxurious prison, Mary Queen of Scots is either a shameless beauty who killed her husband, or the rightful queen of England and Scotland, tragically held captive by Elizabeth the First. But to the dog who loved her, Mary is simply his mistress, and the centre of his life.

While Mary desperately plots to seize both her freedom and the throne, her dog Folly's world is one of chasing mice behind the tapestries and enjoying turkey legs with quinces for supper. Until the day comes when they try to take his Queen away ...

Based on the true story of the dog who was with Mary when she died, *The Dog Who Loved a Queen* is a fascinating tale of religious bigotry, plots and passion — and the unquestioning loyalty of a small Scottish terrier.